A SHIPWRECK
CONSPIRACY

A JUDGE MARCUS FLAVIUS SEVERUS
MYSTERY IN ANCIENT ROME

ALAN SCRIBNER

Torcular Press

Also by Alan Scribner

Marcus Flavius Severus Mysteries in Ancient Rome
Mars the Avenger
The Cyclops Case
Marcus Aurelius Betrayed
The Return of Spartacus
Mission to Athens
Across the River Styx
The Persian Assassin

Anni Ultimi: A Roman Stoic Guide to Retirement, Old Age and Death
With J.C. Douglas Marshall

ISBN: 9798671599404 (paperback)

Library of Congress Control Number: 2020916494
Amazon Kindle Direct Publishing
Seattle, Washington

Dedication
Ruth and Paul

TABLE OF CONTENTS

PERSONAE

Judge Severus' familia and court staff
Marcus Flavius Severus – Judge *emeritus* in the Court of the Urban Prefect and *iudex selectus*
Artemisia – Severus' wife
Aulus, Flavia, and Quintus, their 20, 18 and 12-year old children
Alexander – Severus' freedman and private secretary
Quintus Proculus – court clerk
Gaius Sempronius Flaccus – judicial assessor
Caius Vulso – centurion in the Urban Cohort
Publius Aelianus Straton – *tessararius* in the Urban Cohort
Crantor of Rhodes – former Olympic pankratiast and bodyguard for Judge Severus
Tryphon, Procne – family slaves
Argos – family dog
Phaon – family cat

Lucius Sergius Paullus – *Praefectus Urbanus,* the Prefect of the City of Rome

Persons connected with the ship Andromeda
Septimus Sosius Sulpicius – Judge in the court of the Urban Prefect

Junius Catius Asper – Judge Sulpicius' assessor
Titus Papirius Paculus – Roman of the Senatorial Order
Gaius Paculanus Antipater – freedman of Titus Paculus and owner of the shipping company that chartered the *Andromeda.*
Titus Paculanus Zeno – freedman of Titus Paculus
Demetrios – *Gubenator*, Captain of the *Andromeda*
Claudius Casca – lawyer for Demetrios
Gaius Opimius – owner of the *Andromeda*
Lucius Aemilianus Scylax – *Magister navis*, Shipmaster of the *Andromeda.*
Baaldo – *Proreus*, First Mate of the *Andromeda*
Atrox – chief of a robber band
Aures – 'Ears', a robber

Persons connected with the theft of silk
Ipse – 'Himself' – the arch criminal
Vespilla – owner of an elegant dress shop
Glaukos – a tailor who makes silk clothes for Vespilla
Felix – a recruiter for the robbers and seller of stolen silk
Balaena – The Whale – resident of the *Insula Octavia* and robber
Hector – captured robber

Octavia Priscina – owner of the *Insula Octavia* and the *Insula Priscina*
Persephone – Octavia's private secretary
Ninnius – doorman at the *Insula Prisca*
Furius, Kastor, Borvo – assassins
Lollius – *ianitor*, doorman, at the *Insula Paculus*

The story is set in Rome in the summer of the year 171 CE, 2 years after the events in *The Persian Assassin.*

Roman hours: The day was divided into 12 day hours, starting from sunrise and 12 night hours from sunset. The length of the hour and the onset time of the hour depended on the season since there is more daylight in summer, more night in winter. In the spring and fall, close to an equinox, the hours were approximately equal to ours in length, with the 1st hour of the day at 6-7 am. and the 1st night hour at 6-7 pm.

The events in this book take place in the summer. A day hour can last up to an hour and 15 minutes, while a night hour is correspondingly shorter, 45 minutes.

For simplicity, the equinox times of the hours mentioned in this book are:

1st hour of the day	–	6 – 7 am
2nd hour of the day	–	7 – 8 am
3rd hour of the day	–	8 – 9 am
4th hour of the day	–	9 – 10 am
5th hour of the day	–	10 – 11 am
9th hour of the day	–	2 – 3 pm
10th hour of the day	–	3 – 4 pm
12th hour of the day	–	5 – 6 pm
1st hour of the night	–	6 – 7 pm
2nd hour of the night	–	7 – 8 pm
3rd hour of the night	–	8 – 9 pm
4th hour of the night	–	9 – 10 pm
9th hour of the night	–	2 – 3 am

Ancient Rome

The picture on the left shows the model of ancient Rome in the Museum of Roman Civilization in Rome.

The numbers on the picture locate places mentioned in the book, according to the following key:

1. Forum of Augustus
   Judge Severus' courtroom and chambers

2. Caelian Hill
   a) Severus' *insula*
   b) *Domus* of Titus Paculus
   c) *Domus* of Octavia Prisca

3. Subura
   a) *Insula Octavia*
   b) *Taberna* of Taurus
   c) *Insula Paculus*

4. Esquiline Hill
   Insula Prisca

SCROLL I

I

MARCUS FLAVIUS SEVERUS: TO HIMSELF

I don't believe in the gods, but if I believed in any of them, it would be Fortuna. We may be loath to recognize or admit it, but fortune and chance play an enormous, sometimes decisive, role in our lives.

The prime example I always think of in my life occurred when I was a young student in Athens. I was studying cosmology, the nature of the Universe, at the feet of Epicurean and Stoic philosophers, the former theorizing an infinite Universe composed of atoms and void, the latter a finite Universe that in cycles was born, died in a 'burn out' and then was born again. These ideas were fascinating, but the teachers were somehow not satisfying me. I wanted more.

One hot summer day I happened to be seated in the Stoa of Attalos in the Athenian agora, enjoying the cool breeze blowing through the stoa and thinking about the Universe, when an old man with a long white beard and a cane tripped as he passed my bench.

I went over to help him up and led him to the bench where I had been sitting so he could catch his breath and recover. He thanked me for my help and while recovering from his fall asked me who I was and what I was doing in Athens. I told him, mentioning in passing my problem with the philosophers I was studying with. He said to me that I ought to spend time with the Platonic philosopher at the Academy, Ariston of Athens. He said Ariston was especially interested in the nature of the Universe and I might find him just what I wanted. I thanked him as he got up and left.

I thought about what he had said and a few days later sent a message to Ariston, expressing an interest in studying with him. I was invited to visit his school, which was in his home, and while Ariston showed me around, he told me about some of his students. One of them, he mentioned, was his daughter, Artemisia. He was educating her along with the boys because Plato advocated educating women equally with men as Guardians of his Republic.

Ariston took me into his library and there was Artemisia at the book shelves browsing through a scroll. When she turned around and I saw her, it was like I was hit by a bolt of lightning from Zeus. I couldn't take my eyes off her. When she saw me, she couldn't take her eyes off me. We were both smitten on the spot. From that moment everything in my life and her life changed. Within a short time, we became lovers and then quickly man and wife and eventually parents of three children.

However, if it hadn't been for that man, whose name I never learned, who tripped in the stoa in front of the bench where I happened to be seated on that day at that time, I would never have met my wife. My children would not exist. I would have eventually married someone else, and other children might exist instead. My whole life would have been different.

If that isn't chance, if that is not Fortuna playing a dominant role in my life, I don't know what is. And, of course, many, if not most other people have had analogous encounters with Fortuna, in meeting their spouses, in getting jobs, in encountering friends or foes, in by chance falling into situations affecting their whole lives.

I am not musing about that incident in the stoa for no reason. It is because it has happened to me again. Fortuna has once more emerged into my life. This time she led me onto a path away from my retirement, which I greatly value and even love, to become involved with crimes of murder and robbery I would not even have heard of except by chance.

As it happened, I had come to Rome with Artemisia, and two of our children from our retirement villa in the Alban hills to attend a wedding. We were supposed to return to the country the next day, but because my daughter Flavia wasn't feeling well, we postponed our return. So we all had a few free days to spend in Rome until Flavia recovered.

And it was during those few days in Rome, that by chance I became involved in a sensational criminal case, a conspiracy to beach the merchant ship *Andromeda*, rob its extremely valuable cargo of silks from the country far to the East called *Seres* or *Thina*, and murder anyone who got in the way.

But it was not just the nature of the crime that seduced me away from my retirement. It was the strong suspicion that the wrong man had been convicted and sentenced to death for a crime he didn't commit.

And even more, I soon became aware that behind the conspiracy was a devious, clever criminal. He called himself *Ipse*, meaning 'Himself', the same word applied to Emperors by their courts. Who was this person? I was seduced by my own curiosity to find out.

Why was my curiosity so seductive in this case? To be honest, I don't really know. But a person doesn't always have to know precisely why he does something. I just knew what I wanted to do. Like Socrates, I trusted in my inner *daemon*. Like Aristotle and the Stoics, I relied on my *hegemonikon*, that part of the human *psyche* that has hegemony over him, his ruling faculty, his command center, the small personal portion of universal Reason that resides within him.

I therefore returned to the judge's Tribunal as a servant not only of the goddesses Fortuna and Justitia, but of my own inner *hegemonikon* as well.

II

SEVERUS VISITS HIS FORMER COURT AND HEARS ABOUT A SENSATIONAL CASE

At breakfast in their Caelian Hill apartment the day after the wedding, Severus, Artemisia, the children, 18-year old Flavia and 12-year-old Quintus, and Severus' freedman and private secretary Alexander started to plan the next few days, since they would be 'stuck' in Rome. Two of the family slaves, Tryphon and Procne, and their large black Molossian hound Argos were also with them, but Argos took no part in the planning.

Flavia had told everyone she didn't feel well at all and wanted to stay in bed. She was coughing a lot, though her forehead felt normal, without fever. So everyone else had to decide what to do for the next few days until Flavia recovered. Tryphon and Procne, who were serving and eating breakfast with them, also had to await their instructions for the stay in the city.

While enjoying their usual morning meal of bread, olives, dates and wine a messenger arrived for Artemisia.

"That was fast," she commented while opening the threads of a waxed tablet. She had earlier that morning hired a private messenger service down the street and sent a message to her good friend Valeria who lived on the Esquiline Hill. "Good," she announced to her family, "Valeria wants to have lunch."

"Where?" asked Flavia between coughs.

"At our favorite restaurant in the Forum of Trajan. And then we'll probably do some shopping afterwards. How about you, *deliciae*?" she asked, turning to her husband.

"First, Alexander and I are going to my old courthouse in the Forum of Augustus to say hello to my court clerk Quintus Proculus. Then I plan to go to the gym in the Baths of Trajan and practice my javelin throwing. I'm hoping my coach is still there. I'm out of practice and need to get up to speed again."

"And you?" asked Artemisia turning to Alexander. "You're not going to the gym, are you?" It was a superfluous question. Alexander was not an athlete or ever aspired to be one. He was an intellectual, a master of knowledge, facts and theories, and as excited by liberal arts studies as a fanatic sports fan was by chariot races and gladiatorial combats.

"No. After we see Proculus, and while the judge is throwing javelins, I plan to go to the Forum of Peace to see a new exhibit I heard about at the wedding yesterday."

"What exhibit?" asked Quintus with interest. Though basically a math prodigy, he was always interested in any museum exhibit and always brought the enthusiasm of a precocious young boy to it.

"I heard yesterday that there's an exhibit at the Forum of Peace of giant bones of creatures that once lived here long ago. Dragons, chimeras, griffins and other monsters. Many people think these are mythological animals, but we have their bones and we can see them in museums. The Emperor Augustus once put on a famous exhibition of bones like this. In this exhibit, I heard, there's supposed to be a giant tusk bigger than any elephant's. It was recently found while digging a foundation for a temple."

"I want to go too," said Quintus.

"All right," replied Severus. "You can come along with us to the Forum of Augustus and then we will all go to the exhibit. I would like to see it too. I'll throw javelins afterwards."

"Also, keep in mind," said Artemisia, "we're giving a banquet tomorrow night for all our old team. Vulso, Straton, Flaccus, Proculus and us. I'll send out invitations this morning."

And with that, it was now the 2nd hour of the morning, and so they all finished breakfast. And while Flavia, coughing, went back to bed, Severus, Alexander and Quintus dressed for the Forum of Augustus. Quintus put on his boyhood *toga praetexta*, a toga with a reddish-purple stripe along the hem, just like magistrates wore when in office. When Quintus came of age, he would have to switch to a plain white unadorned toga, just like his father's, who was not a judge at the moment. Alexander, as a freedman of a Roman citizen, was himself a Roman citizen and therefore could wear a toga. But unlike Severus who as an Equestrian and therefore, along with members of the Senatorial Order, an upper class *honestior*, was required to wear a toga in public, Alexander was not and so opted to wear a much more comfortable tunic.

The walk down the Caelian Hill to the forums area proved as congested and difficult as ever. Though no wheeled vehicles were allowed in Rome during the day, still the density of litters and crowds of pedestrians streaming and rushing to their work in the forums or in the central area of the Urbs always created congestion, sometimes with cursing, sometimes leading to altercations, sometimes to fights. Still, Severus, Alexander and Quintus made it to the Forum of Augustus without inordinate delay, arriving shortly before the 3rd hour, the starting time for court sessions. As they entered the Forum of Augustus, they couldn't help but stop to admire the beautiful Temple of Mars the Avenger at the center of the forum. No matter how often they had seen it, its eight gleaming white front columns and beautifully painted pediment sculptures evoked wonder. Pliny the Elder regarded it as one of the two most beautiful temples in Rome.

But at the moment, almost everyone's attention was centering on the colonnade surrounding the forum. Behind the colonnade were judge's chambers and clerk's offices. In front, the 4-foot high Tribunals for judges were being set up in preparation for that day's trials. For from the time of the Republic and continuing during the Empire, all trials, even or especially those where an emperor presided, had to be held in public. The people could then see for themselves what was going on. Governments that held trials in secret simply could not be trusted or relied upon. Public trials were an important part of Roman *libertas.* At least that was the theory and the belief of most Romans.

Crowds of onlookers, court buffs, and hired claques to cheer on or boo various sides in the litigation were beginning to assemble and take seats or standing room in and behind the semi-circular *corona* facing each Tribunal. For the Forum of Augustus was the main venue of the Court of the Urban Prefect and its criminal cases. And criminal cases always drew the most interested and involved crowds.

Severus, Alexander and Quintus walked into the colonnade and entered the portal to his former chambers. "My former court clerk," Severus said to his son, "knows more law than any two judges, more than anyone."

"More than you?"

"Yes. More than me. He's spent his whole life in the courts. He takes down proceedings in Tironian Notes shorthand and knows more law and more precedents from his own experiences in the courts. No one can match that."

A court slave accosted them just inside the portal.

"We want to see court clerk Quintus Proculus," said Severus.

"Judge!" shouted Proculus, who had just seen them enter, "what a great surprise. He came over and exchanged greeting kisses on the lips with Severus and

Alexander. This was the Roman style of greeting for family, close friends and peers. For others, a kiss on the cheek or a handshake was appropriate. "What a sight for sore eyes. And you too, Quintus. My, how you have grown."

"You're a sight for sore eyes too," said both Severus and Alexander. They were all smiles, with glowing eyes and faces, happy to see each other.

"Come inside to your old chambers and sit down. I'll have wine and fruit brought in," said Proculus.

"Isn't there a judge occupying the chambers this morning?" asked Severus as they entered his old chambers and sat down around a table.

"Usually it's Judge Memmius. But he's not sitting today. You remember him. He took over your chambers and his wife stole your beautiful white couch."

Severus smiled ruefully, because he never got that couch back. However, being retired it didn't matter anymore., except when reminded about it.

"Have you come back to watch the big trial going on before Judge Sulpicius?"

Court slaves brought in a bowl of fruit and mixed water and wine and poured each person a glass full.

"No. We came to Rome for a wedding yesterday, but Flavia got sick and we have to spend a few days here until she gets better. But what is this big trial?"

"The shipwreck trial. The shipwreck and robbery and murders on the *Andromeda*. You haven't heard about it? It's a sensation in the Urbs."

"I've been in the Alban hills looking at stars and planets. We don't get the Daily Acts there. We don't hear much about what's going on in Rome. That's one of the advantages of living in the country. But tell me, what is this shipwreck. What was robbed? Who was murdered?"

"I will tell you what we know, though as you will see, it's hardly the whole story. That's what makes this trial a sensation. No one really knows if the defendant is totally guilty or completely innocent. The court buffs on both sides are divided and adamant and passionate."

Severus and Alexander had some wine and sat back to listen. Quintus had some fruit and leaned forward to hear Proculus' story.

"About three months ago," began Proculus, "the merchant ship *Andromeda* sailed from Alexandria bound for Rome. It was a medium size merchant ship, with a capacity of about 500 tons, with a crew of 200 and with 250 passengers. She had a cargo of lentils, wheat, olive oil, wine, Alexandrian glassware and one rare and very valuable item which I will get to in a moment.

"Since it was in the middle of the sailing season, the sea was smooth and there wasn't that much wind. There had been no sudden storms either. Everything was more or less on schedule. But when the ship was nearing Ostia, the port of Rome, having just passed Laurentum, something happened. It was the middle of the night, but instead of keeping to its course toward Ostia, the ship suddenly veered to the right, and headed toward land marked by torch lights on the beach."

"Was there some sort of mistake made? Did they think the lights were from Ostia?" asked Severus.

"Not possible. The main light from the port of Rome comes from the lighthouse flame high above sea level. No. This was clearly not Ostia. But the ship deliberately headed for shore, with its foremast taking in the wind and propelling it onto land. Once on the beach, the prow got stuck in the sand, and the stern got battered by the surf. As a result, the ship broke in two, with the stern falling over to the side. And then, before the crew and passengers could begin to cope with the situation, the ship was attacked by a gang of sword wielding robbers who randomly killed anyone getting in the way. In all they killed over 20 people, both crew and passengers. It was a massacre."

"Clearly," interjected Severus, "the robbery was pre-planned. Robbers were already there waiting for the ship to beach itself and there were accomplices onboard the ship who steered it onto land. This was a well thought out and pre-arranged conspiracy."

"I agree," said Proculus. "But let me continue. The robbers entered the hold of the ship and stole only the one item of the cargo. And what was that item? It was raw silk from *Seres* itself. From that mysterious country far to the east that is surrounded by a wall and that produces the exorbitantly valuable silk."

"How valuable is it?" asked Quintus.

"A good question. Silk from *Seres* is a beautiful, lightweight sheer material, *serica,* that is more valuable than gold. Some women have dresses that cost up to 10,000 sesterces, the equivalent of almost 10 years pay for a Roman legionary. I don't know how much silk was on board the *Andromeda*, but it was probably worth millions.

"When word of what happened reached Rome the next morning, the Urban Cohort and the Praetorian Guard were called out and they searched the hills and area near the shipwreck site. They found a few of the robbers who, after some physical persuasion, I mean torture, confessed to their part in the robbery. However, the leader of the robbers was not apprehended."

"What about the accomplice on the ship?" asked Alexander. "Who steered the ship onto the beach? Who ordered the ship to beach? What was the *Gubernator,* the Captain, doing? What about the *Proreus*, the First Mate? And wasn't there a *Magister navis,* a Shipmaster aboard, an agent of the owner or one of the owners?"

"Now we're getting to the crux of the story," continued Proculus. The ship was chartered and the charterer placed a *Magister navis* aboard. As Shipmaster, he was responsible for the seaworthiness of the ship, of fitting out the ship, of hiring the crew, of maintaining the ship in good shape and of all administrative issues concerning the cargo and passengers. When the ship was at sea, then the *Gubernator*, the Captain, was in charge. But the Shipmaster is missing. He must have been killed or is with the robbers, either as a hostage or as an accomplice. The same is true for the *Proreus*, the First Mate. He is also missing.

"As for the helmsman, the man who controlled the rudders, he was an old man and his body was found on the deck. Clearly, someone had taken his place at the tiller and steered the ship onto the beach."

"And the *Gubernator*, the Captain, the person who commanded the ship at sea. What of him?" asked Severus.

"He is the one on trial for murder and robbery. Demetrios is his name."

"What does he say?"

"He first said that the shipwreck occurred in the middle of the night. He was asleep in his cabin. The First Mate had the watch. The Captain said he woke up when he felt the ship inexplicably turning to starboard and then as he left his cabin to investigate, someone knocked him out from behind. He doesn't know who. He says the last he remembers when he went to sleep is that the ship was heading north toward Ostia. He didn't order the ship to change course and doesn't know who did.

"However, he was subjected to judicial torture and after a while confessed to conspiring with the robbers. Later he recanted and again asserted he had nothing to do with it. He was asleep or unconscious the whole time. But he was tortured again and again confessed."

"Was there any corroboration for the confession," interrupted Severus. "As you know, under Roman law, confessions obtained by torture are suspect and can't be credited without corroboration."

"The prosecution argues he confessed to details of the crime known to be true, and that he couldn't have known them if he was asleep or unconscious."

"But did he confess to any facts that were not known to the authorities. In my mind, it's not real corroboration without that element. Otherwise someone being tortured can be forced to say what he's told to say."

"I agree with you judge. But I don't know all the details of the case. Maybe we can find out because he is on trial right now before Judge Sulpicius, just across the forum. And today is the last day of the trial with the final summations for prosecution and defense."

Proculus flashed a sly smile. "Do any of you want to see what will happen?"

III

SEVERUS ATTENDS A TRIAL

Proculus obtained seats for Severus, Alexander, Quintus and himself in the last row of the *corona*. This accorded with Severus' desire not to be on the Tribunal or in any way associated with the trial. He just wanted to be an unnoticed spectator.

On the Tribunal, a 4-foot high platform with *curule* chairs, camp chairs without back or arms, were Judge Sulpicius, his assessor and a court clerk taking down the proceedings in Tironian Notes shorthand. Against the wall behind the Tribunal were lictors holding *fasces*, bundles of rods symbolizing magisterial power. In the city of Rome, the axe usually in the center of a bundle was removed. A statue of Jupiter Fidius, the god of good faith, stood to the side. It could not be an official Roman court without this statue.

In front of the Tribunal were tables and chairs for the prosecution lawyer and his assistants and for the defendant and his lawyer and assistants. The *corona* of seats behind the litigants was completely full, while behind the *corona* stood a large crowd of court buffs and onlookers, along with claques hired by the competing lawyers to cheer for their side in the case and jeer for their opponents.

Judge Sulpicius was an imperious looking man, with his head held high and an almost arrogant sneer on his face. His beard was in the style of the Emperor. Apparently, he was a recent addition to the panel of judges because Severus had never met him.

"Bring in the defendant," commanded the Judge.

Two lictors led the *Gubernator* to his seat in the court. To Severus he looked worse than a wrecked ship. Haggard, stooping, beaten down and twitching, every step seemingly difficult and painful. He was dressed in a black tunic, its color symbolizing a defendant's distress and ill fortune.

At a nod from the Judge, the prosecution lawyer stood up, took an orator's stance, and with outstretched arm prepared to address the court. It was to be his final summation after days of hearing witnesses and taking evidence.

"Isn't that Septimus Eggius," said Severus to Proculus, who nodded in agreement. "He's a high-priced lawyer. We had him in two cases in the past, didn't we? The Prefect of Egypt's stepson, for one. I wonder who's paying him to convict the *Gubernator* of the wrecked ship."

"You'll also notice, Judge, the lawyer for the defendant, who summed up yesterday, is Claudius Casca, also a high- priced lawyer. He appeared before you in the trial of the bandit Bulla. You might also wonder who's paying him."

The lawyer for the prosecution began his speech to the Judge.

"*Eminentissime*, I stand before you today to refute the absurd claims of the defendant. He alleges that he was asleep or unconscious for the whole time his ship changed course, ran aground and was robbed of its valuable cargo of silk. He didn't see any murders, he didn't hear anyone scream, he was unaware of anything. How convenient! How very convenient!

"But we must never forget that the defendant was the Captain of the *Andromeda*. If he didn't order it to change course, who did? No one else had the authority to give such an order except the *Magister* of the ship. But he is missing, either killed or drowned. Also, we have to ask why would any Shipmaster conspire to have his own ship robbed? It makes no sense. So if the Shipmaster didn't order the beaching of the ship, the only one who could have was the Captain."

Here Eggius pointed at the defendant. "Him. He ordered it. He is the accomplice on the ship of the robbers and murderers waiting on land. Him. The *Gubernator*. The Captain. The Greekling Demetrios.

"And remember, the lame excuse that he was asleep or unconscious that he is foisting on this Court at this trial is not the only story he has told. He also confessed to his crime. He even confessed twice. 'Oh', says Demetrios. 'I was tortured. What I said under torture is unreliable. I confessed to end the pain.' *Eminentissime*, he might have confessed to end the pain, but his confession was true. How do we know that? Because his confession was corroborated, as is required under Roman law. It was corroborated by the numerous details he supplied, all of which have been confirmed as having happened. He confessed that he conspired with the robbers long before the ship sailed from Alexandria. He confessed how it was decided where the ship would beach so that the robbers would already be there waiting. He confessed how he himself handled the tiller and turned the ship onto land. He confessed how he ordered his crew not to interfere with the unloading of the silk. He watched as the robbers stole the cargo of silk and indiscriminately murdered anyone who got in the way, whether crewmen, his own crewmen, or innocent passengers. All these details he could not have known if he were asleep or unconscious.

"Therefore, it is Demetrios the Greekling, Captain of the *Andromeda*, Demetrios the pirate, Demetrios the murderer who is guilty and deserves the highest punishment of all – death. And not an honorable death like beheading, but a painful death like crucifixion or being fed to wild beasts in the arena." Eggius once again pointed at the defendant. "Die, Demetrios! Die cruel murderer! Die vicious robber! Die monster!"

Then the lawyer sat down.

Judge Sulpicius did not retire to his chambers with his assessor to discuss the verdict. Rather, he had already made up his mind and addressed the defendant without leaving the Tribunal. "Stand up and hear the verdict."

Demetrios stood, with lowered head.

"The verdict is that you are guilty." The claque of Eggius' supporters burst into cheers. "Guilty of deliberately wrecking your ship. Guilty of robbery. Guilty of many murders. And the sentence is death in the arena. *Ad bestias*. To the beasts."

The claque cheered again, wildly and longer. When they quieted down, the defendant's lawyer Claudius Casca stood up and announced with indignation in his voice. "We will appeal this unjust verdict and sentence."

"You have the right to appeal, of course," replied the judge. "This is the Court of the Urban Prefect and I am appointed as judge by the Urban Prefect, so you have the right to appeal to the Urban Prefect himself. But the only good it will do you is to delay the execution of the sentence."

With that, while the prosecution claque cheered even more loudly, Judge Sulpicius stood up and left the Tribunal, along with his assessor and court clerk. Eggius stood smiling and triumphant while his claque gathered around him and praised him.

Demetrios was led away by the lictors to a prison cell where he would stay until his appeal was heard and, if he lost, until execution.

Severus turned to Proculus. "Quintus, we are having a banquet tomorrow night at my apartment, to which you are invited. All our old team will be there. Vulso, Straton, Flaccus. We will discuss what just happened then."

He turned to Alexander and his son. "Shall we go see the giant bones?"

They nodded and then headed toward the nearby Temple of Peace.

IV

A BANQUET IS HELD AND
A PLAN IS MADE

After the trial of Demetrios, Severus, Alexander and Quintus went to the exhibit of strange bones at the Temple of Peace. They learned the bones had been found mostly when excavating foundations for temples or buildings or digging trenches to make road beds. Apparently, these strange bones were found everywhere within the Empire, from Rome to Greece, in the East, in the West, in the North, in the South. It was common to find them and they were truly astounding.

No one really knew what they were, but the best opinion of Natural Philosophers was to identify them as centaur bones, dragon bones, griffin bones, sea monster bones, bones of some sort of extremely large birds, even bones of giant men. There was a huge tusk on display in the exhibit, larger than any elephant tusk, which could have been from a Calydonian boar. For people who thought creatures like dragons and griffins never existed and were just mythological, here was proof that they really had existed. The myths were confirmed.

Severus also got to spend time at the Baths of Trajan throwing his javelin on the exercise field. While he was doing that, Alexander and Quintus began a program of visiting various libraries in the Urbs. Alexander wanted to do some research and reading of his own, while Quintus was looking for mathematical and geometry texts that might interest him. There were 28 public libraries in Rome, so their search had to take a while. But they started in the Greek and Latin libraries in the Forum of Trajan.

The banquet in Severus' Caelian hill *insula* started at the 12th hour of the day, while it was still light outside. Caius Vulso and Publius Straton were the first guests to arrive. Both were long time members of the Urban Cohort, Vulso as a Centurion and Straton one rank beneath him, a *Tesserarius*. Both were long time aids to Severus on his cases as a judge in the Court of the Urban Prefect and as a *iudex selectus,* an appointed special judge.

Vulso was a veteran of the legions, having served in the army with the legion I Minervia in Germany and II Traiana in Egypt, among others. After 20 years, he had opted to take his retirement bonus instead of a land grant and came to Rome to enlist in the Urban Cohort. He was a large, strong man, sometimes brutal, but self-educated, clever and experienced. Judge Severus relied on him for his ability to get things done, as much by guile as by force.

Straton had reached the Urban Cohort by an entirely different path. He had been a slave in the Imperial house of the Emperor Hadrian when young and was freed on Hadrian's death. With his sad brown eyes, he could blend in anywhere and go unnoticed and overlooked as an ordinary unremarkable person. He was therefore an expert in taking undercover roles, from a street philosopher to a wagon driver to a devotee of a religious cult to a member of a funeral procession. From his experience of slavery, he retained a certain dislike of Romans, but he was loyal to Judge Severus and a valuable aide in his investigations.

Both Vulso and Straton exchanged greeting kisses with Severus and Alexander and began animated discussions with Artemisia, Flavia and Quintus, renewing old acquaintances and reminiscing.

Next to arrive was Quintus Proculus, Severus' law clerk, and then Gaius Flaccus, who had been Judge Severus' assessor from when he graduated from the law school of Sabinus and Cassius, the same school Severus and his father and grandfather had attended. When Severus retired to the Alban hills, Flaccus became a successful lawyer in the courts of Rome. He had a wicked sense of humor and was smart, incisive and a person whose opinion Severus valued.

When all the guests had arrived, they retired to the *triclinium* dining room and took their places on the couches by the dining table. At the head couch were Severus, Artemisia and Flavia. On the couch on their right were Alexander, Proculus and Quintus, while on the couch on their left were Vulso, Straton and Flaccus.

The dinner was catered by a restaurant nearby and slaves or servants from there began to serve the food. Before the first course, however, Severus' slave Tryphon brought in small statues of the Severus family *lares*, the ancestral spirits of the household, while the family slave Procne carried in a small smoking brazier. Severus sprinkled a small amount of grain, salt and wine on the brazier causing it to sizzle and smoke, while Procne intoned "the gods are propitious." Everyone observed a moment's silence and then the gods were taken out of the room and the meal got underway.

The first course, as was traditional at a Roman meal, was eggs, this time fried with *oenagarum*, a mixture of wine and *liquamen*, a salty fish sauce. This was followed by a selection of sea food patties, oyster patties, mussel patties and fish patties, followed by a patina of asparagus. These were preliminary to Severus' favorite main course, ostrich. Flavored with savory spices, pepper, lovage, and thyme, it was the tenderest of all meats, as far as he was concerned.

The wine was a splendid dry white Falernian, aged 15 years and amber in color. Falernian, Pliny's Natural History noted, was the only wine that flamed up when fire was applied to it.

The conversation centered around the visit the day before to the exhibition of giant bones at the Temple of Peace. Quintus enthusiastically described the gigantic tusk and other remarkable bones he had seen, leading to the conclusion that they must have been bones of creatures which no longer exist, but are described in mythology.

"So there must be some truth in the myths when it comes to animals of past ages," concluded Quintus.

"That's true," added Alexander. "It's as Aristotle deduced when he found sea shells on a hilltop in Greece. He reasoned that at one time that hill had been under water. So also, these giant bones must be of creatures that had once existed but no longer did."

Dessert was then served, grapes, dates, figs and, of course, apples, the traditional ending fruit of a Roman banquet.

And with the dessert, Severus brought up the topic of the trial he had witnessed the day before and the conviction and death sentence for murder and robbery of the Captain of the wrecked ship, the *Andromeda*.

"What did you think?" asked Vulso with an expression as if he knew something about it. "Was Demetrios guilty or not?"

"I don't know," replied Severus. "He confessed, but was tortured into confessing. On the other hand, the prosecution said his confession was corroborated. He knew details of the crime he couldn't have known if he was asleep or unconscious."

Vulso laughed. "He knew them only because he was told what they were and then tortured into saying what he had been prompted to say."

"How do you know that?"

"You may have heard that after the shipwreck was reported, soldiers from the Urban Cohort and Praetorians were sent to investigate and capture the criminals. As a Centurion in the Urban Cohort, I was among them. I commanded a *vexilla* of troops and so I learned what happened, or at least as much as we were able to find out."

"Tell us," said Severus.

"When we arrived on the scene the next morning, we found the ship on the beach, broken in two. It had sailed right up onto the shore, its prow got stuck and the surf battered the stern until it eventually broke off. There were dead bodies everywhere, and not from drowning, but from sword or spear wounds. These were both crew and passengers. The slaughter appeared to be indiscriminate. We interviewed survivors who told us that there were bandits waiting on shore when the ship was beached. In fact, they said, the shore had been marked with torches, as if to tell the ship where to beach. Obviously, this was a prearranged crime. Someone or some people on the ship knew to beach the ship where the robbers were and where they signaled with torches in the middle of the night."

"Did you learn who steered the ship onto the beach?"

"Not really. Who could have done it? There was the *Magister Navis,* the Shipmaster, who on board and in charge of the ship's condition. His name is Scylax. There was Captain Demetrios, the *Gubernator*. Also, perhaps the *Proreus*, the First Officer. His name is Baaldo. He had the night watch and could have done it. But the person in charge of the tiller, an old man skilled in manipulating the two side rudders, was dead of a sword stroke. We weren't able to find the *Magister* or the *Proreus*. They could have been killed with their bodies ending up in the sea. Or they were taken prisoner by the bandits or maybe one or both of them were accomplices of the robbers and went off with the thieves. But while those two officers were missing, we did find Demetrios, the Captain, wandering dazed around the ship. He said he had been asleep and then knocked unconscious when everything happened. Later, he was questioned by the investigating court and since he was a provincial and not a Roman citizen, he could be tortured for evidence. At first. he denied any involvement, but when the torture increased, he confessed. Someone had to pay, and he was available, so to speak."

"Weren't there any survivors from the ship, crew or passengers, who saw who was at the tiller when the ship turned toward the beach?"

"It was the middle of the night and the deck torches had been extinguished. Most everyone was asleep. There were a few crewmen who saw that there was someone at the tiller, but no one could say who. It was just too dark."

"What did the bandits you captured say? What happened to the stolen silk?"

"The bandits we captured were primarily street people from Rome who were recruited to unload cargo. They were brought by *carpentum* coach to a beach and were instructed to enter the hold of the ship and take every bale they could find, and only bales. They weren't told what was in the bales, but they assumed from the weight and feel that there was some sort of cloth inside. Other cargo, like wine, oil, lentils, wheat and glassware were to be left alone. Only the bales of cloth were to be taken."

"Who told them this?"

"Someone they were handed over to at the beach who seemed to be the leader of the bandits. His said his name was Atrox. And Atrox in passing alleged to them that behind the scenes was someone called *Ipse*, 'Himself', who gave the orders. *Ipse*, we all know, is how an emperor's staff refers to him or what the head of a school or of a household is called by their underlings. No one we captured knew this *Ipse*'s real name, or ever met him, or so they said, even under torture."

"And the bales of silk? Did you find any?"

"No. They disappeared entirely. Probably taken to Rome by carriages. Presumably they will eventually appear on the market. They are extremely valuable, after all."

"Do you think Demetrios, the Captain, was guilty of steering the ship onto the beach, that he was an accomplice of the bandits?"

"I don't know. All I know is that his confession is unconvincing to me because the interrogators and torturers essentially told him what to say."

"And, of course," commented Severus. "That is completely illegal. According to the law, the victim of torture should be asked direct questions, not questions containing the answers the interrogator wants to hear. Judge Sulpicius must know this. This torture was a judicial torture, wasn't it? Didn't Judge Sulpicius interrogate him properly, asking direct questions, not leading ones?"

"From what I hear, Judge Sulpicius did ask him direct questions, like 'what happened', but when Demetrios maintained he didn't know, Judge Sulpicius looked the other way and let his assessor, I don't know his name, ask leading questions. He would say, 'you beached the ship yourself, didn't you?' 'You took over the tiller.' Demetrios would say no, but then excruciating pain followed until he said 'I beached the ship myself. I took over the tiller.' Then Judge Sulpicius would ask 'what happened?' And Demetrios would say 'I took over the tiller and beached the ship myself.' That's what I heard happened here," Vulso concluded.

"Who did you hear this from?"

"I heard it from one of the Urban Cohort soldiers who heard it from one of the lictors, who was present during the torture session."

"Hearsay, then. Double hearsay."

"Yes, hearsay. But probably true."

"Then if the confession is bad, what evidence is there against the captain?" asked Flaccus. "Nothing to show whether his story of being knocked unconscious, convenient as it appears to be, is either true or false."

"And if that's the case," concluded Severus, "under the law, the burden of proof has not been met. According to the Rescript of Antoninus Pius, the burden of proof lies on the one who asserts, not the one who denies."

"So Demetrios should have been acquitted," continued Flaccus. "Not convicted. Is that what you are saying?"

"I don't see how any other conclusion could be reached."

"What is to be done, then?" asked Flaccus.

"There will be an appeal to the Urban Prefect. He must be made aware of the situation."

"And who is to make him aware?" asked Flaccus.

Everyone looked at Severus. He caught their looks. "Me? I'm retired. I'm *emeritus*."

"Well, suppose you were to handle the investigation," interjected Artemisia. "What would you do? How would you go about finding *Ipse*, for instance?" she asked, slyly goading her husband on.

"First of all, there are two aspects of the crime that have to be explained. One, the robbers were waiting with torches at a specific place, knowing in advance that the ship would see their signal and beach itself there. Two, the ship beached itself at a specific place knowing in advance that the robbers would be there and signal to the ship. This means there was a shipwreck conspiracy with one or more conspirators on the ship and other conspirators on the shore.

"How was this done? Who arranged it? Because it was obviously pre-arranged. The robber chief Atrox alleged there was some mastermind who gave him his orders. He called him *Ipse*. If there was such a person, was it *Ipse* who conceived the plan to deliver the ship and its rare cargo into the hands of waiting bandits? If so, *Ipse* is at the head of the conspiracy and therefore our prime target."

"Second, I would try to find the Shipmaster Scylax and the First Mate Baaldo."

"But they're dead, aren't they?" questioned Alexander.

"I don't know that. Maybe they are dead. If so, nothing can be learned from them, except that they were probably not conspirators. But since you're asking my opinion how to make progress, I would assume they're alive and see if they can be found. Moreover, if they are alive, why aren't their whereabouts known?"

"Because they're in hiding," suggested Straton.

"And if they're in hiding," continued Severus completing the idea, "it must be because they are part of the conspiracy. Maybe if we find them, they can lead us to *Ipse.*

"Third, we should investigate where the silk went. It must be somewhere. Probably in a warehouse or storeroom somewhere. Theft of the silk was the main object of the conspiracy, after all. So, we should try to find the silk."

"If you were in charge of the investigation?" proposed Artemisia. "If this were your *cognitio*? How would you go about it?"

Severus didn't like the direction these questions were taking. But he enjoyed answering them.

"Artemisia, my *deliciae*, I would put you in charge of finding out about the silk. You and Alexander, who I would want to go to silk shops and libraries to learn about the silk trade. I would want to know as much as possible about where the silk comes from, how it's produced, how it reaches us, why it's so valuable and anything else of interest.

"I would assign Flaccus, Vulso and Straton to see if they could locate the *Magister navis* and the First Mate on the one hand and *Ipse* on the other.

"As for myself, I would have to speak to the Urban Prefect and get myself appointed either back on the panel of judges or a *iudex selectus*, a special judge for this investigation. The Urban Prefect will need someone to do this because there will be an appeal to him personally from the convicted Captain Demetrios and he must know what really happened before he can decide the appeal."

Severus turned to Flaccus. "I'm retired. Perhaps you can take on this *cognitio*."

"Not me. I'm too busy with my law practice. I can help out somewhat, but I can't lead the investigation. So it looks like you're elected, judge."

"I'm retired, as I said." But he said it unconvincingly. His interest was provoked; his juices were starting to run; his desire for action and solving problems was still a force within him.

"You're not retired anymore," replied Artemisia, picking up on her husband's feelings. "We've just decided that the captain should have been acquitted, didn't we? So how can you stay retired until this miscarriage of justice has been corrected?"

"A miscarriage of justice, perhaps. But why am I responsible for correcting it? The judicial system is not perfect. There may be many miscarriages of justice. Am I condemned to be some sort of demigod, a servant of Justitia avenging every miscarriage?" It was a last-ditch objection.

"Not every one of them," shot back Artemisia. "Only those that Fortuna contrives for you to encounter."

Severus picked up on his wife's feelings, realizing that when he said he would put her in charge of the hunt for the stolen silk, it must have started her juices flowing too, if they hadn't been started already.

Everyone else looked at Severus, nodding in agreement to the idea that he should take the *cognitio* for the crime. Their juices had started to flow too with Severus' mention of their roles in a new investigation.

Severus closed his eyes and thought in silence. He had to admit to himself that that as much as he loved retirement, he was still excited by action. And then, also, he wanted to solve this crime. Why? He couldn't in the moment articulate all the reasons to himself. But he knew it was not entirely because there might be an innocent man wrongfully convicted. There were other factors involved. One was the challenge of ferreting out *Ipse,* the criminal behind the whole scheme. Severus had to admit to himself that the identity of *Ipse* intrigued him. His own curiosity was getting the better of him.

This was the way his *hegemonikon*, his inner ruling faculty, was telling him what he must do, what was right for him. And this feeling of what he must do was strong and clear. He must enter the case. If he didn't, he knew he would not be at peace within himself. It was a matter of understanding who he was and of being himself.

He opened his eyes and with a faint smile announced his decision. "I'll send a message to the Urban Prefect and ask to meet with him tomorrow."

Everyone raised their glass of wine in a toast, shouted *felicitas* for good luck, and drank.

SCROLL II

V

SEVERUS MEETS WITH THE URBAN PREFECT

After an exchange of messages, Severus presented himself at the Praefectura building the next day at the 4th hour, the time the Urban Prefect, Lucius Sergius Paullus, had agreed to see him.

The Urban Prefect was one of the highest and most important posts in the government. He was responsible for the good order of the city of Rome and was the chief magistrate of the Court of the Urban Prefect, the court Severus had served in for years. He was also in charge of the Urban Cohort, the military body in the city of Rome tasked with ensuring law and order in the Urbs and within its 100-mile jurisdiction.

Severus had met Paullus only once, on the day two years before when he took himself off the panel of judges and retired. At that time Paullus was newly appointed as Urban Prefect, having replaced Quintus Junius Rusticus, with whom Severus had worked productively on a number of occasions. Paullus had been born in the province of Asia, was a member of the Senatorial Order, as all Prefects of the City of Rome had to be. He had wide governmental experience, having been a consul and a proconsul of the province of Asia.

Severus was shown into Paullus' office by an aide and exchanged greeting kisses on the lips with the Prefect.

"It's a pleasure to see you once again, Severus. Have you heard from the Emperor recently?"

Paullus knew that Severus was a personal friend of Marcus Aurelius and had been a friend of the Emperor as a child. That was long before Aurelius had been selected by the Emperor Hadrian to be trained as a future emperor and adopted into the Imperial family.

"No, *clarissime*," replied Severus, using the 'most illustrious' honorific for members of the Senatorial Order. "The Emperor as you know has been on the German frontier with the army since last Fall, and I haven't heard from him since then."

"Let's hope he can wind up the war there soon. In any event, Severus, what can I do for you?"

"I happened to be in the Urbs a few days ago to attend a wedding and when by chance my daughter became ill, we decided to stay in the city for a few days until she gets better. So I went to my old court to visit old friends and chanced to see the end of the trial of Demetrios, the captain of the ship *Andromeda*."

"Yes. I have been following that trial, as has just about everyone else. A terrible affair. Murders, theft of a fortune in valuable silks from *Seres*. But at least we've caught most of the culprits. And the Captain confessed, and yesterday he was convicted and sentenced to death in the arena. Terrible. The whole affair is terrible."

"It may become even more terrible because I heard from one of my former police aides with the Urban Cohort, who was one of the commanders of the troops sent to catch the robbers, that the confession of the Captain is flawed. It was obtained under torture and under circumstances making it untrustworthy. The Captain may not be guilty at all."

"How is that possible? Wasn't the torture judicial torture? Wasn't it done under the supervision of Judge Sulpicius? I'm sure he conformed to the rules. We know that evidence from torture is weak and dangerous, but not to be rejected entirely. And in any case, there was corroboration of the confession, wasn't there? That's what I've heard."

"That's just it, Prefect. I've heard that the details of the crime, the corroboration if you will, were fed to the Captain when he said he was innocent and then extracted from him under excruciating torture. He was in effect told what to say. That is not corroboration, of course. And without the confession, there is no evidence against the Captain, so the burden of proof has not been met."

"If what you say is true, Severus, that must be corrected. I understand there will be an appeal to me personally as chief magistrate of the Court of the Urban Prefect. Clearly then, I will have to investigate the matter of the Captain's guilt more fully when the appeal is brought before me.

"I must say, though, that what you were told is hard for me to believe. Until proven otherwise, I have to presume that the confession was obtained correctly, that he was not fed answers and that there was satisfactory corroboration."

Severus looked directly at the Prefect. "I would like to investigate the matter prior to the appeal. I do not want there to be a miscarriage of justice. I have served Justitia all my life and I still believe in serving her even when retired. I would rather go back to my retirement home in the Alban hills, but once having become aware of this possibly terrible miscarriage of justice; I feel compelled to see that justice is done."

Severus knew he was being somewhat tendentious in giving his reasons. They weren't false, but it wasn't the whole story. He felt he couldn't just tell the Prefect that he and his wife and his staff were excited by the prospect of getting back into action. That was too personal. Nor could he say that his inner *hegemonikon* was telling him to take on this case. That was even more personal. But further reasons were unnecessary because the Prefect was compliant.

"Would you like me to appoint you one of my assessors for the appeal? Your skill in solving criminal cases is well known. As my assessor you can solve the case and help me out on the appeal. You can whitewash two walls with one bucket, as the saying goes."

"Thank you for welcoming me as an assessor, but I don't think it will do. To properly investigate the case, I will have to have the power to compel witnesses, to hold court, to direct police forces. Only with the magisterial power of *imperium* can I do that. So I would have to become a judge again. I would have to be either on the panel of judges or become a special judge, a *iudex selectus*, and assigned the *cognitio* of the shipwreck of the *Andromeda,* its robbery and the murders."

"Since the case is now on appeal from Judge Sulpicius' verdict," realized the Prefect, "his *cognitio* has expired. So it would be possible for you to be appointed to take over the case."

"Besides," added Severus, "even if this Captain is guilty, there is still the question of who conspired with him, because surely there were many accomplices on land, and perhaps more than one on the ship. Who are these criminals? Where are the stolen silks? The conviction of the Captain, even if guilty, is only part of the story, and perhaps only a small part."

"All right, Severus. I will appoint you *iudex selectus* to solve the case of the shipwreck of the *Andromeda* and all its ramifications. That will clearly include getting to the bottom of the Captain's guilt or innocence. You can work out of your old chambers in the Forum of Augustus, if you wish."

"I would want that, yes. And I also would want my police aides, Vulso and Straton, my former court clerk Quintus Proculus and my previous assessor Gaius Flaccus to be assigned to help me."

"Consider it done."

Severus was about to get up to go, but the Prefect had something to add.

"There is one more thing you have to consider. Whoever is behind this massacre of sailors and passengers on the ship will stop at nothing. He is already responsible for many murders and presumably will not forego another murder if he thinks your investigation becomes a threat to him."

"Are you saying that my life will be in danger?"

"Yes. That's precisely what I'm saying. So I would recommend you have a bodyguard. I can assign one to you, if you like."

"I think a bodyguard may be a good idea. Better safe than sorry. But I can hire one on my own, in any case."

"As you wish, Severus. And good luck."

"Thank you, Prefect."

Later that day, Severus spoke to Vulso about a bodyguard.

"We can hire Crantor of Rhodes, the Olympic pankratiast. You will remember him from our case of the return of Spartacus. He was your bodyguard for a while then."

"Yes. I remember him. Mild mannered and totally confident. Is he in Rome? Can we get him?"

"Yes. He and I have become friends since that case. He lives in Rome and now trains pankratiasts. I had dinner with him just a few days ago. He's perfect as a bodyguard. A pankratiast in the Olympic games in Greece. A winner at the Greek games in Rome during the Floralia festival. A master in fighting. Pankratiasts, as you know, are all-in fighters where everything is legal except biting and gouging the eyes out. That's in the arena. Outside the arena, there are no restrictions at all."

"Hire him."

That night in bed with Artemisia, Severus recounted the day's events and mused about the workings of Fortuna.

"If it hadn't been for Flavia becoming sick, we would have returned to the Alban hills after the wedding and I would never have attended the trial of Demetrios."

"Flavia is not sick."

"Not sick? What do you mean? Is she better?"

"She never was sick. Her cough was a fake."

"What are you saying? Why would she fake being sick?"

"This morning I spoke to Procne about Flavia. She said that the first day here, Flavia told her and Tryphon that her friend Pudentilla was coming to visit and they could take the whole day off. So they did. Then yesterday and today the same thing happened. But today, they returned early and found that it wasn't Pudentilla who was visiting Flavia, though she might have been here earlier, but her so-called brother Bellerephon."

"Bellerephon? The boy who Flavia said she was in love with when she was 15? As I recall, he's a slave, isn't he? A child of slaves in the household of an Equestrian in the *insula* across the street, though raised and educated as a son by his master."

"That's exactly who I mean. Well, now she's 18 and she's seeing him again. And possibly more than just seeing him."

"I hope she understands that she can't marry him. It's illegal for a slave to marry, and any child they may have together would be considered illegitimate.

And not only that, what about the law from the time of Vespasian 100 years ago saying that any woman who sleeps with someone else's slave should herself be treated as a slave. Flavia can't want that."

"She understands all that, of course. But apparently that isn't stopping them from being together."

"What are we going to do?"

Artemisia rolled over and embraced her husband, reaching her hand under his tunic. "I don't know what we're going to do about her. But I do understand love and passion and therefore I know what we're going to do."

She pulled off her own tunic, while Severus pulled off his.

Then they embraced and made love.

VI

ANTIPATER, THE CHARTERER OF THE *ANDROMEDA*, IS INTERVIEWED

The man seated across the table from Severus, Alexander and Proculus was husky, toga-clad and confident. He announced his name as Gaius Paculanus Antipater. "I am a freedman of Senator Titus Papirius Paculus." A small ingratiating smile accompanied his declaration. His demeanor was lively and intelligent. He gave the impression that he missed nothing and no one could put anything past him.

Antipater had brought with him two slaves, who were seated in the anteroom of Judge Severus' judicial chambers, and a *capsa*, a cylindrical case holding scrolled documents.

"I have all the legal documents in here, *eminentissime*" he said, careful to use the judge's Equestrian honorific in addressing him, while pointing to the *capsa*. "The documents show that the ship *Andromeda* belonged to the Ostia shipping corporation of Opimius and Caecilius and that my shipping company, which is called by my name, G. Paculanus Antipater, chartered *Andromeda* on the Ides of May. The charter was in order to ship cargo of wine, *terra sigilata* pottery, glassware and other trade goods to Alexandria and return to Ostia with a cargo of oil, lentils, wine, wheat, Alexandrian glass and silk. These items were destined for my company's warehouses in Ostia, eventually to be sold in Rome."

Proculus leaned toward Severus and said into his ear, "*Lex Julia Repetundarum.*"

Severus recognized the reference. It was to a 200-year-old law passed during the Republic that contained as one of its provisions a ban against members of the Senatorial Order owning ships for profit. The law was still in effect. It theoretically confined senators to more 'honorable' businesses like agriculture, while opening the door to members of the Equestrian Order and others to make huge profits from merchant shipping. However, the law was easily circumvented by senators having their freedman or other agents technically own the ships in their name, while the senators reaped the profits. This is what happened here, Proculus was saying by his reference to the Republican law.

Severus nodded to his court clerk and looked back at Antipater. "We understand that you chartered the ship in your name and that your company was established in your name to circumvent the law barring senators from owning ships for profit. But Senator Paculus is the real owner, correct? He is the real *exercitor*, the person to whom the profits go, right?"

Antipater started to protest. "No, *eminentissime*, I chartered *Andromeda* in my name for my profit. I head a company engaged in mercantile shipping, among other businesses. The Senator has nothing to do with it. I have all the documents here and I…"

Severus held up his hand. "I don't want to argue about it. So let's move on. Antipater, who finances these voyages? Who pays for the charter, the crew, the cargo?"

"My company finances most of it. We also borrow money from bankers – *argentarii*, and professional business investors – *negotiatores,* and then we have private investors as well."

"When you chartered the ship, did you also pick the officers, like the *Magister navis* Shipmaster, the *Gubernator* Captain, the *Proreus* First Mate?"

"I picked my own Shipmaster and I picked my own First Mate. The Captain, the *Gubernator*, Demetrios, came with the ship, as did the crew."

"I understand that your selections, the *Magister* and the *Proreus* are missing. The ship owner's Captain, we all know, has been convicted and is awaiting death in the arena."

"That is correct, *eminentissime.*"

"It occurs to me that this is lucky for you, isn't it?" asked Severus. "After all, if the Captain supplied by the Ostia merchant corporation is responsible for wrecking the ship, not your Shipmaster or First Mate, you may be legally off the hook for loss of the ship and its cargo."

"The ship corporation is contesting that, *eminentissime,* because the charter contract makes me responsible for the ship and the cargo and doesn't say anything about blame. Nevertheless, our position is as you say. My company, the charterer, should not be responsible for the loss of the ship, if the owner, Opimius, through his chosen Captain, caused the shipwreck."

"And the cargo, the silks, who bears that enormous loss?"

"I claim it is Opimius, because his corporation owned the ship and he supplied the shipwrecker. I claim that the ship owners must bear the loss of the ship themselves and also pay me damages for the stolen silks. Opimius, of course, takes the opposite position, saying that under the contract of charter I must bear the loss of both the ship and the cargo. Eventually, it will be decided in the courts, though it may take years to resolve the litigation. However, as of now, I have a huge loss."

Severus, Alexander and Proculus were thinking the same thing and there was no need even to say to each other what they were thinking. Here was a strong motive for the charterer to blame the Captain for the shipwreck.

"Did you hire Eggius, the lawyer to prosecute Demetrios? Are you paying his fee?"

"*Eminentissime*, Judge Sulpicius selected Eggius and I don't see the relevance of…"

Severus interrupted him with a hostile glare and a sharpened voice. "I determine the relevance, not you. Answer my question."

"Yes, *eminentissime*. I am paying the lawyer Eggius. Just as Opimius and his shipping company is paying Demetrios' defense lawyer Casca. But in my case, it is to see justice done."

"Justice, yes," replied Severus, looking straight into Antipater's eyes. "I'm also here to see justice done." Severus' expression was some combination of sinister and ironic. Antipater looked away.

"Now, Antipater, tell me about your Shipmaster and the First Mate?"

"The *Magister* Shipmaster was Lucius Aemilianus Scylax. He was a very experienced seaman and had worked for my company for years, as he had for other shipping companies in Rome. I have often used him as my representative aboard my chartered ships, as *Magister*."

"You say he was experienced. Who else did he work for?"

"He worked for Opimius, the owner of the *Andromeda*. at least once that I know of. He also worked on ships of Zeno, one of my major competitors."

"Can Scylax handle the helm? Does he know how to steer a ship?"

"I don't know that specifically. But I wouldn't be surprised if he could. Scylax can handle most posts on a ship. But with him as *Magister*, I can feel secure that the ship will be in good shape for its voyages. Better shape than when I chartered it. That's his specialty and most important job, after all."

"Why didn't you make him Captain of *Andromeda* when you chartered it?"

"I would have, except the Opimius, the owner of the ship, insisted on having his own Captain in charge when the ship was on the sea. That way he feels secure that his ship is in good hands. Unfortunately, in this case he didn't know that his Captain had conspired with robbers to beach the ship and steal my cargo."

"If that's what occurred," said Severus.

"That's what he was convicted of," replied Antipater.

"That's what he's appealing from," shot back Severus.

"In any case," answered Antipater, "*Magister* Scylax is missing, obviously killed during the robbery."

"If he were still alive, where would he be?"

"He would have reported in to me and told me what happened. The fact that he didn't proves to me that he is dead."

"Maybe so. But maybe not. I can think of other explanations. Where does he live?"

"He lived in an *insula* apartment house in the Subura."

"Where?"

"Not far off the Clivus Suburanus, about half-way up the Subura. The *insula* is a normal 4-story apartment building. It's called the *Insula Octavia*. A distinguishing feature is instead of having shops or *tabernae* on the ground floor, it has a small temple to *Magna Mater*, the Great Mother, on one side of the entrance and a small Jewish synagogue on the other. You will have no trouble finding it."

"Now tell me about your First Mate."

"The *Proreus* was named Baaldo."

"Baaldo? What kind of name is that? Carthaginian?"

"Could be, but in his case it's Phoenician. Baaldo is from Sidon, reputed to be the home of the best sailors. He's worked on my company's voyages for a number of years. And like Scylax, he also worked on ships owned by Opimius, the owner of *Andromeda*, and by Zeno, one of my major competitors. I'm sorry he's dead."

"As with Scylax, how can you be sure he's dead?"

"As with Scylax, he would have reported back to me if he were alive."

"Where does he live in Rome?"

"He lived in the same *insula* as Scylax."

"Who was the helmsman on *Andromeda*? Who controlled the side rudders?"

"An old man, a member of the crew. An experienced helmsman. I don't remember his name, but I know his body was found, killed by a sword cut to the abdomen."

"So, it's possible that the helmsman was ordered to steer the ship onto the beach and when he objected, he was killed and a conspirator with the robbers then handled the tiller and beached the ship."

"Yes. That's what Demetrios did."

"If he did it. I have one last question, Antipater. Who do you think committed this crime?"

"I can tell you right now who did."

"Who?"

"It was Titus Paculanus Zeno. Like me, a freedman, a former slave of Senator Titus Paculus. And like me, an entrepreneur in business. A former partner. We started out in business together. But now he is my arch rival and he hates me. He's behind this crime."

"You mentioned this Zeno before as someone both Scylax and Baaldo had previously worked for."

"That's right."

"Why does Zeno hate you? Why did you two fall out?"

"It was over a woman. Cassandra. She was also once a slave of Paculus. Zeno wanted to marry her, but she married me instead. He thinks I stole his woman. He will never forgive me and always tries to injure me. He did it."

"Besides this animus against you, do you have any evidence that Zeno was involved in this crime?"

"No. But I'm sure you'll find evidence against him because he did it. And come to think of it, *eminentissime*, there is one other person who might be behind this crime against me."

"Who is that?"

"Opimius."

"The owner of the ship? Why would he beach his own ship and rob it?"

"For money, of course. For the silks. And for one other reason. He hates me. He wants to see me fail."

"Why is that?"

"Because I am outcompeting him. He was once the premier merchant shipper. Now I am. And we don't get along personally."

"Then why did you charter the *Andromeda*? It is one of his ships."

"Business necessity. My ships were in use when this business opportunity to buy the silks happened. You see, we never know when or where a shipment of pure *serica* will arrive from the far East. It sometimes comes by the land route through or around Persia, arriving at Antioch in Syria. And then sometimes it comes by a sea route from *Seres* to India and then from India to Alexandria. When this large shipment of pure silk arrived in Alexandria, my agents there knew to buy it up. But I needed a ship to bring it to Rome and the only one available at the time was the *Andromeda*, owned by Opimius."

"I see. All right, Antipater. You can go now. I'll probably need to ask you more questions when I've reviewed the documents you brought."

"I am at your service *eminentissime*." With that, Antipater wiped his brow, collected his two slaves from the anteroom, and left.

When he was gone, Alexander began the comments. "We should send someone to that apartment house in the Subura to see what they know about the Shipmaster and First Mate."

"Just what I was thinking," replied Severus. "If they're alive and Antipater knows it, we can't trust him to tell us where they are. He has an interest in not wanting them found. It might undermine his claim against the owners of *Andromeda* and make him responsible for loss of the ship and the cargo. Even if Antipater doesn't know where they are, if those officers conspired with the robbers, they themselves would probably be in hiding."

"So what do we do?"

"We assume they're both alive. If they're alive, they can be found. And I agree we should start at that *insula* where they once lived. Let's have Straton assume one of his undercover roles and go to that apartment house. He may find out something useful."

"I'll send for Straton right now," said Proculus who got up and wrote out a message to be delivered to Straton at the Urban Cohort headquarters in the *Castra Praetoria*.

"And there's something else," added Severus. "I want to know who the investors in the voyage with the silks were. The *negotiatores* professional business investors, the *argentarii* bankers and also any private investors. All of them would have a strong motive to have Demetrios convicted, just as Antipater does. Investors hardly want to lose their investments. Maybe their names are in the documents left here, so we'll have to go through them thoroughly.

"Next," he instructed his court clerk, "get Vulso and Flaccus. I want them to question the robbers who were captured. They must know things we want to know about how the crime was committed."

A few hours later, Flaccus, Vulso and Straton showed up at Severus' chambers and they discussed their missions for the next day.

When Straton arrived, they discussed his undercover mission to the apartment building where both Scylax and Baaldo lived

"I suggest," said Straton, "that I pretend I'm one of the crew of the *Andromeda* who survived. I could say the ship's officers had told me to look them up when I was in Rome. Let's see how that works."

"All right," replied Severus. "It sounds like a good idea. But I want you to have someone in the vicinity who can protect you if you run into trouble."

"Who?"

"I'll lend you my bodyguard, the pankratiast Crantor of Rhodes. I don't think I'm in any danger, at least not yet, so he is available to back you up."

"Good idea. I don't want to end up being beaten up, like what happened to me in our case of the body on the steps of the Temple of Mars the Avenger, when I was pretending to be a philosopher."

Severus called in Crantor, who was seated in the anteroom. He was larger than most men, though not excessively so, but his tunic barely contained his muscles. He had a strong face and moved like a cat. His manner, like many totally confident athletes, was mild and polite. Together, they planned Straton's undercover penetration of the *insula* where the officers of *Andromeda* lived.

Next Severus turned to Flaccus and Vulso, who had arrived at his chambers. "Tomorrow I want you both to question the robber captives who are being held in prison awaiting execution in the next Games. I want to find *Ipse*. Find out anything you can. What his real name is. What he looks like. Where he can be contacted. Whatever you can find out will be useful. You can promise leniency to anyone who cooperates and you can promise extra horrible deaths for those who are uncooperative. I want *Ipse*.

"Also, I want to know anything you can find out about how the bandits came to be at the beach waiting for the *Andromeda* to run aground. When they were told about going there, when did they arrive, who told them, what they did with the silks they took off the ship, *et cetera*."

"We understand," said Flaccus. "We'll start in on them tomorrow morning."

"Finally," said Severus, "there's one other thing I have to do. I want to find out more about Antipater and about Zeno, the person he accuses of committing the crime."

"Who from?" asked Vulso.

"I think from their patron, the person whose freedmen they were, Senator Titus Papirius Paculus. I want to speak to him tomorrow. Proculus, send a messenger to the Senator, tell him I need to speak with him and unless he can suggest a better time, I will be at his house tomorrow at the 4th hour."

Severus then turned to Alexander. "Alexander, have you finished your research into the silk trade. Are you ready to report to us about it?"

"I am."

"Good. Artemisia spent today at the silk market on the Vicus Tuscus, talking to silk merchants. So then tomorrow morning, first thing, before we head out on our various missions, we'll all meet here at the 2nd hour to hear Artemisia and Alexander report about the silk trade and the mysterious country far to the east where silk comes from."

Everyone nodded their agreement.

That night Severus briefed Artemisia on the day's events.

"After my report tomorrow morning, *deliciae*, can I actually start looking for stolen silks?

"You can start tomorrow. Have you talked to your friend Valeria about helping?"

"Yes. She's eager. It will be like the time we went to the Market of Trajan together to look for glassware and talk to a suspect in the case of the synagogue murder and theft of the golden chalice."

"Will you be Artemisia? Or Elektra?"

"Elektra. It's my undercover persona in your investigations, after all. I will be a rich Athenian woman visiting Rome and put on my thick Greek accent when speaking Latin."

"Remind me."

Artemisia began to sweet talk her husband with Greek accented Latin, where every starting vowel was preceded by an 'h' sound. "Hi want your harms haround me," mimicked Artemisia. "Hi want to kiss your heyes and your hears." They both began laughing, but then Artemisia brushed her long hair over her husband's body and they quickly turned from laughing to loving.

VII

ARTEMISIA AND ALEXANDER
REPORT ON THE SILK TRADE

The next morning at the 2rd hour, Severus, Flaccus, Vulso, Straton, Crantor and Proculus gathered in the judge's chambers to hear Artemisia and Alexander report on the silk trade.

Artemisia had spent some time the past two days asking questions at the Vicus Tuscus silk market, while Alexander had done research in several libraries in the City. Between them they had information the judge and his associates would find useful and interesting.

Two tables were set up in the judge's chambers. A long table with wine and fruit in the middle where everyone sat, Severus at one end and Artemisia and Alexander at the other. To the side was a smaller table with two articles of shiny, off-white material displayed. When Severus signaled to begin, Artemisia stood up and walked to the smaller table, pointing.

"Here is how we receive silk from *Seres*. Either in fabric rolls or in bundles of threads. When we look for the stolen silk from the *Andromeda*, we will be looking for material in either of these forms.

"The threads are primarily for weaving into thin cloth and then into clothes which are then dyed with vibrant colors, as we've all seen. This silk from *Seres* is the most comfortable, strongest, lightest and most durable of any material we know. It is also the most expensive, comparable in value to gold, diamonds, pearls, emeralds. Silk is priced by its weight and often a pound of silk is worth a pound of gold. Even more if it's dyed purple, say. A single pure silk *stola* can cost tens of thousands of sesterces. So few people can afford clothes made entirely from silk."

"You can say that again," snorted Vulso with a degree of anger. "A Roman legionary makes 1,200 sesterces a year, so one of those *stolae* you just mentioned cost more than the salary of ten 10 soldiers for a year. But who is really more valuable? Just try holding up a silk *stola* to ward off a barbarian attack."

"It doesn't seem right, does it?" replied Artemisia. "But that's the way it is." She shrugged and continued.

"While pure silk clothes are not affordable for most people, a lot of clothing nowadays has silk added to wool or linen, to lighten and embellish the toga, or the tunic or the stola. Most of our summer clothes have silk added to make them lighter and cooler. And these are affordable for many."

Everyone at the table nodded their heads and automatically fingered the light summer clothes they were wearing, confirming what Artemisia had just said.

"Also," continued Artemisia, "silk is used for ribbons, parasols, wedding garments, theater canopies, military standards and banners, medical sutures and other articles almost too numerous to list."

"Do you have any all silk clothes?" asked Vulso.

"No," replied Artemisia. "They're too expensive."

"You are members of the Equestrian Order," shot back Vulso, looking at Severus, "surely you can afford them."

"Maybe so," answered Artemisia. "But we both adhere to the Stoic principal of *frugalitas*. We see no need to be extravagant in anything. Linen or wool clothes, with silk added, is sufficient for us."

Everyone understood. Artemisia continued.

"Each silk bolt contains about 20 square feet of fabric. It's used primarily for drapes, awnings, theater canopies, military flags and standards, garlands, wreaths, you name it. We've all likely heard of the Triumphs of Caius Julius Caesar 200 years ago, when he replaced all the linen awnings on the parade route with canopies of silk to stretch over the spectators. The spectators all loved it, but the soldiers complained that the fabulous cost would have been better spent on them rather than on the showy display. In any case, this is what we're looking for, either bolts of rolled silk or bundles of threads."

Artemisia sat down and Alexander stood up to deliver his report.

"We all want to know where this silk comes from and how it's made. However, our information about both these things is limited, often confused and contradictory. But this is what I found out, so far.

"As to where it comes from, we call the land *Seres*, because the silk is called *serica*, or vice versa, I don't know. But the country is located far to the east. This is what we learn from those who bring it to us by a land route. But the people who actually bring it to us themselves don't know much because the silk is passed along from one group of people to another, starting in *Seres* itself. Apparently, there are numerous intermediaries. Whatever the case, *Seres* is located far to the east, beyond India, beyond Bactria, beyond a barrier of extremely tall mountains."

"How long does it take to get from its origin to us?" asked Proculus.

"That depends on the route. There's a land route and a sea route. As to the land route, there's a lot we don't know, although we know some things about segments of it. By land, it takes about 100 days for a caravan to cross Persia, 50 days to cross Bactria, and more days, I don't know how many, to get from those high mountains to Bactria, and some more to get from the Persian border to Antioch in Syria. But that's already 5 months just across Persia and Bactria. How far it is beyond the high mountains to *Seres* is what we don't really know.

"And by the way, these are not small caravans, but often about 600 camel loads, with 10,000 silk rolls, amounting to 4 tons of silk, worth about 16 million sesterces.

"Also, if there are disturbances along the route, like wars, there may be serious interruptions. For instance, during the recent war between Persia and ourselves, the land route had to divert north of Persia, if it was not halted altogether. So often the flow of silk is not steady. It comes when it comes."

Alexander took a sip of wine and then continued.

"We have a better idea of travel time by the sea route, at least the part from India to Italia. This is because there are about 120 Roman merchantmen that sail each year from Egypt to India and back, taking advantage of the monsoons to aid their voyages. The merchant ships deliver trade goods to India and pick up trade goods, like silk, to bring back to the west. The return voyage sails from India to Egyptian Red Sea ports. There, the cargo must be transferred by land to Alexandria, where it is loaded aboard ships, like the *Andromeda*, to sail the Mediterranean to Ostia. This whole journey between India and Italia takes about 4 months.

"And by the way, Pausanius the geographer, in his recent book, says those who bring silk to us by ship, by way of India, call the land of the origin *This*, and its major city *Thinae* or *Thina*. Other sources for sea voyaging sometimes refer to the country not as *Seres*, but as *Thina*. How long it takes by ship from *Thina* to India, I haven't been able to find out. Also. I don't know whether there is one ship that goes from *Thina* to India or whether there are intermediate transfers along the way, like on the land route."

Alexander took another sip of wine and then switched topics.

"As to how *serica* silk is made, again we don't know. We know that on the island of Cos in the Mediterranean they produce what we call wild silk, *bombyx*. It's silk-like, but not as good as true *serica* silk. *Bombyx* is produced by moths, whose cocoons are unwound. But we don't know what *serica* is produced from because it is of a different quality than silk from Cos. Some say *serica* silk comes from trees, some say it's from plants, like linen or cotton. Pausanius says it doesn't come from trees or plants, but like wild silk from Cos, it is made by an insect. However, he says the *serica* insect is twice as large as a beetle and has eight legs, like a spider. It makes its webs in trees, and it's from these webs that *serica* is produced."

"That makes some sense," commented Flaccus. "Spider webs are very fine, after all."

"Which silk, the wild silk or the *serica* silk makes the best see-through clothes?" asked Vulso. "I'm interested because one of my concubines likes to wear see-through clothes for me."

"That must be enticing," commented Straton.

"It is," replied Vulso. "Sometimes even more enticing than no clothes at all."

"Sheer see-through garments," replied Alexander, rolling his eyes at the question, "can be made from either *bombyx* or *serica*, but I suppose silk from *Seres* is always best. I hope that answers your frivolous question."

"Frivolous?" replied Vulso, with a laugh. "You wouldn't say that if you saw Licinia in her see-through tunic."

"To return to *Seres* itself," continued Alexander, "we know very little about it beyond the fact that the country is the source of silk. It is rumored, however, that not just its cities, but the whole country is surrounded by a wall."

Alexander sat down and Artemisia spoke up.

"A basic fact about this raw *serica* silk is that when it arrives here it is already worth a fortune and when it is woven into clothes and dyed it is worth an even greater fortune. There is no other product in the world more desired but about which less is known than silk."

VIII

JUDGE SEVERUS MEETS
SENATOR PACULUS

At the 4th hour, as arranged, Judge Severus arrived at Senator Paculus' *domus* on the Caelian Hill, not too far from Severus' own luxury *insula*. Though dressed in his full magistrate's toga, Severus declined to take a litter, but rather walked the short distance to the senator's house, along with Alexander.

The exchange of messages the day before found the senator's staff fully prepared for the visit and when Severus arrived, Senator Paculus politely came to the front door and greeted the judge with a kiss on the lips. He then led Severus inside and straight through the atrium into his *tablinum* office. Paculus sat down on one side of a desk, motioned to Severus to sit across from him, and pointed to the wine and fruit on the table. There was also an elegantly decorated cylindrical ivory dice throwing cup on the table.

Severus took a sip of wine and studied the Senator. Paculus was younger than Severus by maybe

10 years and looked energetic and intelligent, though there was an air of dissipation in his face. He wore his beard short and curly, in the style of the Emperor, as did most prominent figures, including Severus. The Emperor set the style. And even though Marcus Aurelius was put off by flattery and imitation, it hardly stopped anyone from flattering or imitation. It was, in fact, normal.

"It's a pleasure to meet you," said Paculus. "I understand you're newly appointed by the Urban Prefect as *iudex selectus* to investigate the *Andromeda* affair."

Severus nodded affirmatively.

"Therefore," said Paculus in a brash way, "I deduce that your reason for wanting to talk to me has to do with my freedman Antipater, who chartered the *Andromeda*,"

Severus again nodded in agreement, encouraging the senator to go on.

"Presumably you want to know whether he is a front for me, legally chartering the ship in his name so that as a member of the Senatorial Order I will not run afoul of that old Republican law restricting senators and ships."

Again, Severus simply nodded.

"Antipater, my freedman, actually charters ships on his own. He is a master at business. I don't compare with him in that regard. I don't even know how much he owns, in buildings of his own, in businesses, in slaves, in numerous enterprises he conducts. He is like Trimalchio, the character in Petronius' *Satyricon,* who also was a freedman starting with nothing, who made a fortune on his own. Trimalchio is Antipater's hero. He says so himself. I know he makes a fortune and not just because he brags about it to me.

"He even gives me money to show me his supposed superiority. He says he is giving me 50% of all he makes because I freed him, because I gave him the opportunity to do whatever he wants, to be independent. He also says the money he gives me will pay off my debts. He knows, you see, that I have gambling debts. I love gambling, but sometimes it happens that I lose."

Paculus stopped and picked up the dice cup, lovingly rolling it in his hands. "Do you like to gamble, judge?" He didn't wait for an answer. "There are three dice in this cup. I'll bet you right now that I'll throw a higher number than you."

"I don't care to bet," replied Severus. "I don't find gambling interesting at all."

"You've never bet on anything? Even on chariot racing? Or gladiator bouts? That's hard to believe."

"I have occasionally bet on the outcome of a *latrunculi* game I've played with players in the park. But then I'm a very strong *latrunculi* player and since it's a game of pure skill, I'm betting on my skill, not on some event over which I have no control."

"But that's just the point of gambling. It's the randomness of the outcome. Anything can happen. The wins are exciting, even glorious. They bring you to the heights of experience."

"And the losses?"

"They bring you to the depths. The lows, the agonies, are as important as the highs."

"Do you like the agony?"

"I'm not sure, to tell you the truth. I hate the feeling of deep despair, but I know that without it, the heights of excitement and elation could not be experienced."

"It's not for me. I'm interested in the game, not the money. At the chariot races, for instance, I'm a fan of the Reds and I want to see them win. But if I bet on the outcome, it ruins the race for me. Any focus on the money interferes with my real focuses, the race itself and my team."

"Come on, judge. Just this once. Let's bet. Say, 1,000 sesterces."

"No."

"Any amount, then. You name it. Maybe 1,000 sesterces are too low. How about 10,000 sesterces."

"You'd bet that amount on one impetuous throw of the dice?"

"Absolutely. The more money the greater the emotions, the higher the ups, the lower the downs."

Severus shook his head in a negative gesture, expressing disbelief. However, he wanted to get on with his questioning and not become sidetracked. "All right," he said finally, "one throw apiece."

Paculus' eyes lit up. "How much? 1,000 sesterces? 10,000?"

"1 sesterce."

"1 sesterce? What kind of bet is that? That's nothing."

"You said you wanted to bet and I could choose any amount. I say 1 sesterce. Live up to your word, senator."

He gave Severus a scornful look, rattled the dice box and threw the dice. They came up a 2, a 4, and a 4. "Beat 10," said Paculus smugly, putting the dice into the box and handing it to the judge.

Severus rattled the dice and threw them. It came up a 5, a 6, and a 3. "14," said Severus. "You owe me 1 sesterce."

"I don't have such small change on me."

"I'll wait. Now let's get on with it. You were talking about Antipater giving you 50% of his earnings."

"Yes, that's what he says. I don't believe he's giving me 50% of his earnings. Nowhere near. But it doesn't matter to me. He is trying to convince himself of his superiority to me, but we both know he'll never do that. He is, after all, a freedman, a former slave, a *humilior*, while I am a member of the Senatorial Order, an *honestior*."

"That is only a legal superiority in a society with class distinctions, as we both know. But what about mental superiority? What do you say about that?"

"I say he is very clever, astute and without morals. But I am cleverer and more astute."

"What about morals?"

"I have just as many as he does."

"Can you tell me anything about the *Andromeda* business? Did he ever discuss it with you?"

"Yes, of course. He bragged about how much money he would make on this shipment. Silk from *Seres*. One of the most expensive items there is. He even got me to invest my own money in the cargo. He said I would make a huge profit. He said he wouldn't have to give me any money in the future. I would be fixed for life. But now that I lost my investment, I dislike him even more. If possible."

"Tell me about Zeno, another of your freedmen."

"Zeno? What does he have to do with this?"

"Possibly nothing. But he is a business rival of Antipater."

"Yes. But not only a business rival. They once were partners, you know. They fell out over a woman. Cassandra. She was very beautiful young girl with red hair and green eyes. She was my slave. Also my concubine until I tired of her. Then she seduced both Antipater and Zeno. They both wanted her, so I made them throw dice for her. Antipater won. There's been bad blood between them ever since."

"I see. Well, I think you have answered all my questions, some even without me having asked them." Severus stood up to go.

"Then the interview is finished?" asked Paculus, also standing up.

"Let's say it is finished for the moment. But I may want to continue it later on."

"Maybe you'd like to throw the dice one more time? C'mon, one more time."

"No," said the judge firmly and then turned and walked out.

IX

STRATON AND CRANTOR INVESTIGATE AN APARTMENT HOUSE

Early the next morning, Straton and Crantor found the *insula* they were looking for. As Antipater had said, the entrance was between a small Jewish synagogue and a small Temple to Magna Mater. The building was an ordinary 4-story apartment house, seemingly in fairly good condition. There was a sign over the entrance with a faded painting of a goddess that said 'Insula Octavia'. There was a slave *ianitor*, a doorman, tall and skinny, at the entrance, next to the vat containing feces of the residents waiting pickup for later use as fertilizer. As Straton and Crantor casually ambled by, they smelled the feces from the vat penetrating into the street, causing them to hold their noses and pick up the pace. The doorman had to stay where he was, though he held a bag of rose petals to his nose. It might help cover the smell, although it could hardly eliminate it.

Straton and Crantor scouted the area around the *insula*. They found a *taberna* across the street from the *insula* entrance and took seats from where Crantor could keep an eye on the apartment building. They both had a drink of *mulsum*, white wine with honey, and then Straton headed back to the *insula*. He was dressed in an old gray tunic and went barefoot, as all sailors did aboard ship and many did on land. He held his nose as he started to speak to the doorman, who obligingly came out into the street to hear what the visitor wanted.

Straton came directly to the point. "My name is Straton and I was a crewman on the ship *Andromeda* that was shipwrecked. Have you heard about it?"

"Of course, who hasn't. Not only that, but two of that ship's officers live here."

"I know. That's why I'm here. Both of them, Scylax and Baaldo, told me if I'm ever in Rome I should look them up. So here I am. Are either of them here? Could you tell them I'm here?"

"Wait here. I'll see."

The doorman went into the building and headed upstairs. He returned after a few minutes with two large scruffy looking men, both dressed in ordinary brown tunics. Neither their tunics nor their persons looked particularly clean. Straight off, they maneuvered Straton against the wall of the *insula*.

"Scylax and Baaldo aren't here," one of them said. "And who are you? Why do you want to see them?" The other added. The tone of both men was harsh and threatening.

"As I told the *ianitor*, my name is Straton and I was a crewmember on the *Andromeda*. I'm here to see one of my ship's officers, either Scylax or Baaldo. Is either of them here? I know they'd want to see me."

"They're not here. Come back this afternoon. Then we'll see."

"Thanks. Remember, I worked in the hold below deck. They said I could look them up when I'm in Rome. I'm in Rome but have no job after the shipwreck. Maybe they can find me a new ship. They must have a new ship, no?"

"You talk too much. Come back later this afternoon. Then we'll see what's what."

Straton squeezed between the two men and headed back to the *taberna* where Crantor was still seated, watching.

"I almost came to the rescue," said Crantor, "but I saw you coming away on your own."

Straton filled him in on what happened. They then left the *taberna*, wandered around the Subura idly looking into shops, had lunch at a Subura restaurant, and then returned to the *insula*.

The same two men were waiting for Straton outside the entrance.

Once again they pushed him against the wall of the *insula*. "There are a number of sailors from the *Andromeda* living here. No one knows anyone crewman named Straton. No one knows you."

"I don't know which crewmen you asked. There were almost 200 crewmen aboard *Andromeda*. No one crewman knows every other crewman. Ask the officers, Scylax or Baaldo. They know me."

"As we said," replied one of them, "no one knows you." He began shoving Straton harder. "Who are you?"

Straton protested again, but both of them started to rough him up, pushing him harder.

At that point, Crantor came up and from behind and grabbed both of the men by the scruff of their necks. "What are you doing to this poor fellow?" he said, while dragging them off Straton, twisting their necks so that they faced each other and then banged their heads together. Quicker than Straton could grasp, both men were on the ground unconscious.

"Let's go," said Crantor and they went.

"I've never seen anything like that," said Straton. "What did you do?"

Crantor smiled. "You've only seen pankratiasts like me fighting other pankratiasts in Greek Games. In the arena, there is a certain amount of equality among contestants. But untrained ruffians, *grassatores*, as the Romans call them, aggressor street thugs, like those two have not the slightest chance against an Olympic athlete, a professional like me. Not only am I much stronger and much faster, but I know all the holds and throws pankratiasts train in. They have as much chance against me as a mouse has against a cat. Less even, because a mouse can often scuttle away from the cat. Anyway, Straton, I thank you for your appreciation of my skill. But I have to tell you that I am no match for the current Olympic pankration champion, Demestratos Damas. He is the best in the world and has been for the last five years."

"I don't know about Demestratos Damos. I do know you were very impressive," said Straton. "Very impressive indeed."

"What were they hassling you about?"

"They said no one knew me."

"That means they checked with someone who should know about the crew. Maybe other crewmen?"

"I don't think so. As I told them there were almost 200 crewmen, so any one crewman wouldn't necessarily know all the others. But I told them that I knew the officers Scylax and Baaldo and they knew me. So it stands to reason that they checked with one or both of them."

"Which means one or both of them are alive and in the Subura."

"Precisely."

"Won't the judge be pleased to hear that."

"I'm sure he will. So let's go tell him right now."

A short while later Straton and Crantor arrived at Judge Severus' chambers and told him what happened at the *Insula Octavia* and what their conclusion was.

"I think you're right. Either Scylax or Baaldo or both are alive and well and holed up somewhere not too far from their old apartment house. If they had been there, it wouldn't have taken those two men a few hours to ask them about you. Likely then they are somewhere else."

"So how do we find out?"

"Either a massive raid by soldiers of the Urban Cohort. Vulso can organize that. Or have someone watch the building from outside. Or install a spy into the building, maybe as a tenant."

"I like the spy idea best," said Straton. "It's too bad I can't be that spy, but I know someone who can do it."

"Who's that?"

"A slave with the Urban Cohort who accompanied me in the case of the Persian assassin, when I visited the snake charmers of the Marsic cult in the Apennine Mountains. The slave is named Pectillus and he was willing to take on a dangerous job as long as he was given his freedom for doing it. I think this is just the thing for him."

"Get him," said Judge Severus. "We'll insert him into that *insula* and see what transpires."

"And as for watching the building," added Straton, "maybe we can use Ceionius again, who we met in the case of General Cyclops. You'll remember he was once a Centurion who got an Ignominious Discharge along with everyone else in the disgraced and disbanded Legion XXII Deiotariana. He became a beggar. We've used him a few times to sit outside buildings begging, but really observing for us."

"Doesn't he hold up a placard with a picture of a shipwreck to create sympathy and encourage alms?"

"Yes. A shipwreck placard would be perfect for this case, judge. We can have him sit down begging on the street of the *insula Octavia*."

"Get him."

"One question, though," asked Crantor. "How will they, or we, know what Scylax and Baaldo look like?"

"Antipater, the charterer of the *Andromeda*, knows. So we have to send one of those portrait painters to him. One who can make a realistic picture based on a description, adjusting the face until a recognizable one comes out. We've used one of them a number of times before."

"I'll arrange it," said Straton. "With paintings of the officers, we'll know if Scylax or Baaldo ever come in or go out of that *insula.*"

X

ARTEMISIA AND VALERIA GO SHOPPING FOR SILK

To Artemisia and her friend Valeria, there was one place to start tracking down the stolen silk. And that was an exclusive dress shop, of which there were quite a few in Rome. There were some in the Vicus Tuscus silk market, others in the Market of Trajan and the Saepta Julia market, more on the Via Lata – Broadway, and others in other parts of the city wherever wealthy women lived and shopped.

The two friends discussed the possibilities and decided to start with the shop of Vespilla on the Esquiline Hill, near where Valeria lived. It was a favorite of Valeria's and she was known there. Artemisia, making good use of her mimicking ability, as often in the past would take on the role of a rich Greek woman visiting Rome. As in the past, Artemisia became 'Elektra', speaking her native Athenian Greek with no accent and Latin with a put-on thick Athenian accent.

It would be interesting and fun, not to mention that it would be a shopping trip where anything they bought would be paid for by the government. What could be better?

At the 5th hour the next day, the two women were carried to the shop of Vespilla in a six-bearer litter and were received at the entrance by three bowing and scraping slaves of the store, one very handsome young man and two subservient young girls, who saw the litter arriving. Vespilla herself then came out of the store to greet her customers.

"Valeria," she gushed when she saw the women alite from the litter. "How nice to see you."

Valeria and Vespilla exchanged greeting kisses and then Valeria introduced Elektra, her good friend from Athens who was visiting Rome and wanted to see the shop that Valeria had been telling her about.

"I am pleased to meet you, Elektra," said Vespilla pleasantly.

Elektra, speaking Latin with a pronounced Greek accent where every starting vowel of a word was preceded by an 'h' sound, responded to Vespilla's greeting. "Hi ham very pleased to meet you too, Vespilla."

She and Vespilla then exchanged greeting kisses and Vespilla invited them into the shop where she looked Elektra over with a practiced eye, assessing her for styles and fashion.

Both Valeria and Elektra looked beautiful, elegant and rich. They were about equal in height and had similar long dark hair and deep brown eyes. Elektra's body was thinner and sleeker, Valeria's more voluptuous. They could be and sometimes were mistaken for sisters. Both were dressed in stylish and expensive tunics. Valeria's was red with a green belt; Elektra's was blue with a yellow belt. Both wore beautiful necklaces, Elektra's with amethyst and gold beads, Valeria's with beads of turquoise and gold. The fingers of both women were decorated with several rings of silver and gold.

Vespilla was a handsome older woman, shorter than her two customers, with green eyes, a slim figure and a ready smile. She was dressed in an elegant tunic made of fine linen, though not so fine as to be seen through. Vespilla's tunic was green with orange geometric designs on the hem and sleeve ends, and she wore an orange belt. The green on her tunic enhanced the color of her eyes. She also was decked out in an expensive jeweled necklace and rings.

Vespilla's shop was well appointed. Beautiful rugs from Persia graced the floor, highly polished metal mirrors were strategically situated around the store, mannequins wore designer quality tunics and *stolae* dresses. The lighting was soft, coming both through the newly invented and expensive glass windows and from traditional standing candelabras scattered throughout the store.

"Elektra only wants your finest tunics to take back to Athens," explained Valeria. "And also something special for an elegant party here in Rome."

"Would Milesian wool suit you?" asked Vespilla, motioning to a shop girl, who quickly brought out some tunics and a Roman *stola* of fine wool. Of the tunics, some were so thin as to be almost see-through, while others were denser and more sober. The *stola* was also sober.

"Try these on," said Vespilla, and motioned to one of the slave girls to escort Elektra to a dressing room. She soon came out clad in a yellow tunic with a red belt and displayed herself to Vespilla and Valeria.

"Beautiful," said Vespilla, sizing her up. "It fits so well and you look so beautiful in it."

"It's nice," commented Valeria, without much enthusiasm, "but maybe she should have something finer."

"Hi hagree," said Elektra.

"The only material finer than Milesian wool is, of course, silk. I have some beautiful wild silk from Cos."

"Hi'll try one hon," said Elektra.

"Do you want one, as Seneca said, that reveals to the public what most women reveal only to their lovers?"

They all laughed. "Perhaps not that fine," said Elektra. "But has comfortable has possible hand has light hand silky hon the skin has you have."

The slave girl took Elektra back to the dressing room and brought her a selection of tunics made from the wild silk of Cos.

Elektra now appeared in a light green tunic with a dark green belt and modeled it.

"Also beautiful," said Vespilla.

"How does it feel?" asked Valeria.

"Very nice," said Elektra. "But you know hi once wore ha silk tunic made hof silk from *Seres*. There his nothing like real *serica.*"

"Do you have any dresses of *serica*?" asked Valeria.

"Unfortunately not," replied Vespilla. "It's very rare these days. And extremely expensive. As much as 10,000 sesterces for a *serica stola*."

"Hextremely hexpensive? My husband will hobject. But fortunately, hi have money hof my own," laughed Elektra. "Yes, hi want *serica*. The price doesn't matter."

"Then perhaps we should try another store, Elektra," suggested Valeria. "The silk market should have a dress shop with *serica*.

"If we don't find any *serica*, Vespilla, we'll come back here. But we should shop for what Elektra really wants."

Vespilla took Valeria aside by her elbow and whispered something into her ear.

"Really?" exclaimed Valeria in a low voice, and then even lower said to Vespilla., "Could you have a *stola* ready in three days, because that's when the farewell party will take place. Also we'll take enough raw *serica* to make two tunics, which Elektra's own tailor in Athens will sew."

Vespilla nodded affirmatively.

"Come Elektra. We can go now."

The customers exchanged farewell kisses with Vespilla and left.

Back in the litter, Artemisia asked what the whispering was about.

"She knows where to have real *serica* made into a *stola* and enough raw *serica* for two tunics ready in three days. She wouldn't say where it's from, but we can make a good guess, can't we?"

"Success. Let's go and tell my husband right now."

Valeria stuck her head out of the curtains of the litter. "Change of plans," she said to the litter bearers. "We're going to the Forum of Augustus."

XI

VULSO AND FLACCUS GRILL CAPTURED ROBBERS

While Straton and Crantor were in the Subura, Artemisia and Valeria were shopping for silk and Judge Severus was talking to Senator Paculus, Flaccus and Vulso presented themselves at the Mamertine prison. It was one of a few prisons in the City. In Rome people were held in prison only awaiting trial or sentencing or exile or execution. Prisons were not places that people were sentenced to; they were just temporary holding places.

Six of the captured bandits were there now. A few others were in other prisons. Most of the bandits had escaped, although no one could be sure how many there were because the shipwreck and robbery took place in the middle of the night, in the dark.

Vulso identified himself and Flaccus to a guard. "Which one looks to be the weakest, the one most likely to crack and give us the information we want?"

"I don't know," replied the guard, "though if I were to start in on one, I would take Hector."

"Why Hector?"

"He seems the most distraught, the most rueful. Try him. But every one of them has already been tortured and has spilled out his guts. So I don't think you'll find out anything we don't know yet."

"Bring Hector out," ordered Vulso. "Maybe we'll find out something, maybe not. But if we don't try, we'll get nothing."

The guard quickly appeared with a bedraggled, wan looking, thin man, who was half-naked in a torn brown tunic clotted with blood. His face looked like death itself. He was also still suffering from the pain of torture, as was evident from difficulty in breathing and constant wincing with pain whenever he moved. The guard shoved him into a chair across a table from Vulso and Flaccus.

"My name is Gaius Sempronius Flaccus, and I'm the assessor to Marcus Flavius Severus, the *iudex selectus*, who is investigating the *Andromeda* affair and who is in charge of your fate. If you cooperate with us, you may receive leniency. If not, you will be subjected to an extra horrible death."

"I want to cooperate," said Hector, with a glint of hope in his eyes. "I shouldn't be here at all. It was only because I had no money. I couldn't get food for my wife and children. I had no job. I had to take anything I could get. They recruited me off the streets of Rome. They told me it was just to unload cargo from a ship. I didn't know I would be part of a robbery. I didn't know anything. I didn't murder anyone. Please help me. I shouldn't be here. Please help me."

"I will help you, if you'll help me," replied Flaccus in a gentle voice.

"I'll help you. I want to help. I told everything to those vipers who tortured me, but they didn't believe me. I don't know why. I want to cooperate. I want to tell the truth."

Flaccus replied with an understanding, sympathetic tone of voice. "Then tell me, who recruited you? Where and when?"

Hector had no hesitation in talking. "It was Felix, at least that's what he called himself. I was begging on a street corner in the Subura. He came up to me and said I was lucky to meet him. He needed workers, he said, to unload merchandise at night and he would pay well. I said 'how much' and he said 100 sesterces. Well, 100 sesterces are almost a month's pay for a regular worker. Begging, I may not see 100 sesterces in a year. So I said I was interested. He said 'come with me' and he took me to an *insula* somewhere in the Subura where I was questioned by someone else, who called himself Ballaena."

"Ballaena? A whale?"

"Yes. And he looked like a whale too. He was grossly fat. He must have weighed as much as four men. He had rolls of fat on his face, his neck, his stomach. He was unpleasant to look at. But I answered his questions about who I was, where I lived, what my health was, was I married, did I have children, how long had I been a beggar, *et cetera.* He said the job would probably be five days from then and I and other workers would be transported to where the job was and told what we needed to know then. He then paid me 20 sesterces on account and said I would get the other 80 when the job was completed.

"He then told me I was to meet Felix five nights from then, at the 4th night hour, at a *taberna* in the Subura, owned by an ex-gladiator named Taurus. I don't know exactly where it is, but….."

Vulso held up his hand. "I know where it is." The *taberna* and Taurus were well known to Vulso. The *taberna* and its owner had played a part in the case of the murder victim found on the steps of the Temple of Mars the Avenger. Taurus also had been useful in the search of the Subura in the case of the murder at the synagogue and the stolen chalice. "Go on," said Vulso.

"So I met Felix at that *taberna*. He was already there when I arrived and there were also a few other men around him. Felix put me and the other men into a *carpentum* coach waiting outside.

"We were driven for what seemed like several hours to a small house, I don't know where, and told we would be unloading a beached ship. We would only take bales from the hold, nothing else, and put them in waiting coaches for transportation somewhere else. We then followed men with torches and swords and at a signal we all descended on this beached ship that was broken in two. I saw by the torchlight that people were being cut down by the men with swords, clearing a path. I was led into the ship's hold and told to take out these bales and put them into waiting vehicles. I went in and out of the hold a few times.

"When all the bales were removed, the coaches drove off and I and some other men were left stranded there and told to make it back to Rome ourselves by foot. While we were walking back the next day, we were picked up by soldiers of the Urban Cohort. I told them just what I'm telling you. But I was tortured for more information. I don't know anything else. Then I was brought before a court. I don't know what court it was or who the judge was. I had no lawyer to defend me. I barely got a chance to say anything myself. Before I knew it, I had been sentenced to death in the arena. Why? What did I do wrong? I'm a poor beggar. I haven't even received the 80 sesterces I was supposed to get."

"Do you really expect to get that money?"

"Actually yes. Felix said that when the cargo from the ship is sold, we would all be paid off, the stevedores and the robbers. He even said when and where."

"When and where?" asked Vulso with added interest.

"The Ides two months from then, he said. At the same *taberna*, the *taberna* of Taurus where we met that day. Felix said he would personally give us all the money we were owed. We were to go to the *taberna* of Taurus on that day. Someone would be in a room upstairs with the money. We were only to say the code word 'Ajax' and we would be taken upstairs and paid off. But it was probably just a lie."

Hector broke down and cried. "How did this happen? I didn't do anything bad. Please help me."

"What does Felix look like?"

"He is a big, scruffy looking man, but nothing like the Whale. I don't know how to describe him. He had a short military beard. Felix also talked with a lisp and had a Greek accent. I could point him out if I saw him again. Please, can you help me?"

"Perhaps," said Vulso. "Is there anything else you can tell me? For instance, did you hear anyone mention the name *Ipse* at all?"

"*Ipse*? Himself? Yes. During preparations for removing bales from the beached ship, I heard the name *Ipse* mentioned a few times, as if he was the leader of the robbers, the person who gave orders what to do. But I never met him or heard anything about him other than his name. I don't know if he was present at the beached ship or not."

"What about the *insula* you were taken to by Felix? Can you find it again?"

"I don't think so. It was just one of countless look alike *insulae* in the Subura, which is teeming with look-alike *insulae*, but I think both Felix and the Whale lived there. I know the *insula* was somewhere off the *Clivus Suburanus*, but I'm not all that familiar with the Subura, so I don't know where it is or how to find it. I would help you, if I could, but I can't."

Flaccus and Vulso got up to leave and headed toward the door.

"There is one thing, though, that I noticed. Maybe it will help."

"What is that?" asked Vulso.

"When I left the *insula* after the interview with the Whale, I wanted to go back to the city center, but I turned to the right and someone told me I was going in the wrong direction. I should go to the left. Anyway, on the right of the entrance I noticed there was a small temple to Magna Mater and when I went to the left, I passed a small synagogue next to the entrance of the *insula*. Maybe that will help because most *insulae* have shops or *tabernae* on the ground floor, not places of religion."

Flaccus and Vulso looked at each other, both realizing the same thing at the same time. That was the description of the *insula* according to the ship charterer Antipater, where both the Shipmaster Scylax and the First Mate Baaldo lived. Now it comes up as a headquarters for the robbery of the ship.

How interesting!

When Flaccus and Vulso reported this news to Judge Severus, he called a conference asking Straton, Crantor, and Proculus to join them.

Artemisia was already there to report on what she and Valeria had found out at Vespilla's dress shop. When she finished her account, it was quickly decided that she should return to the shop, along with Judge Severus in his magistrate's toga and Vulso in full battle gear. They would then confront Vespilla and persuade her to reveal her supplier of silk.

Then they turned their attention to what was learned from the captive Hector about the *insula* in the Subura.

"We should raid that *insula*," suggested Vulso, "the *Insula Octavia*, and round everyone up. Arrest everyone and question them all."

"How many people might live in that *insula*?" asked Severus, looking at Straton.

"I don't know. It's a 4-story apartment building, so maybe 30 to 50 people, I would think."

"Let's find out. Straton, that proposed spy of yours, Pectillus? I want to postpone that tactic for now. Instead, I want to send a *Vigiles* firefighter into the building with two soldiers of the Urban Cohort. He is to identify himself as an inspector from the local *Vigiles* firefighters, sent to see that all the apartment houses in the area are properly equipped with fire-fighting equipment, axes, water buckets, *et cetera*, and to inspect all the apartments for safety. In doing so, he is to find out about every person who lives in that building. He should talk to as many as possible and find out who is not there at the moment."

"Good idea," everyone agreed. "We can then get an idea of what we're dealing with in that *insula*," commented Flaccus. "Maybe find Felix and the Whale."

"Maybe even Scylax and Baaldo," added Straton. "Though I doubt it."

"All right," concluded Severus. "Straton, arrange for the *Vigiles* fire inspector first thing tomorrow morning and select two soldiers to accompany him. Vulso, organize a raiding party. After we find out who's in there, we'll be prepared to raid the place at a time when we might catch as many people as we can."

Severus stopped to think to himself and then voiced his thoughts out loud. "The *Insula Octavia* is where two officers of the *Andromeda,* Scylax and Baaldo, and two of the planners of the robbery, Felix and the Whale, all lived. It's a good bet, then, that the conspiracy was either hatched in that *insula* or developed there.

"And as for *Ipse*, he may live in the *Insula Octavia* or he may not. We don't know. But whatever the case," Severus smiled with a broad grin and held up his index finger for emphasis, "now that we're on to his conspirators, we are on his tail. We now have a way to track *Ipse* down."

SCROLL III

XII

GAIUS OPIMIUS, THE OWNER OF THE *ANDROMEDA*, AND THE LAWYER FOR CAPTAIN DEMETRIOS SEE JUDGE SEVERUS

The next morning a messenger arrived at Judge Severus' chambers with a waxed tablet requesting a meeting. It was from Claudius Casca, the lawyer for the convicted Captain Demetrios. It asked if Casca and Gaius Opimius, the owner of the *Andromeda*, could see the judge. It said they had information the judge would want to know.

Severus had his court clerk write back on an empty page of the waxed tablet that Judge Severus could see Casca and Opimius that afternoon at the 9th hour.

The two men arrived promptly at the 9th hour. The lawyer Casca was a large man with a double chin, a pot belly, a belligerent lower lip and a mellifluous voice, brimming with latent power. He was a member of the Senatorial Order and he and Judge Severus greeted each other with a kiss on the lips. A handshake with Opimius, an ordinary citizen, was sufficient.

Once seated around a table, Severus addressed Casca politely using his senatorial honorific. "It's a pleasure to see you again, *clarissime*." The reference to a previous encounter was to the time Casca had appeared before him as a lawyer for the defendant in the theft and murder at a Jewish synagogue.

"A pleasure to see you again, *eminentissime*. And may I introduce my client Gaius Opimius, the owner of the shipwrecked *Andromeda*."

Severus wasted no more words and addressed Opimius. "I was told that ship *Andromeda* was owned by the company of Opimius and Caecilius. Where is Caecilius?"

Opimius was a short man and like his lawyer had a pot belly and two chins. His voice, though not nearly as impressive as Casca's, was nonetheless strong and positive.

"He is no more," answered Opimius, "but I keep his name in the business to honor him and assure clients."

The judge looked at both men, one after the other. "What information do you have for me?"

The lawyer answered in a confident voice. "Judge, we know you have been appointed *iudex selectus* to investigate the case against Demetrios and we are here to tell you he is innocent, the victim of a grave miscarriage of justice."

Casca stopped for effect.

"I'm listening," said Severus.

"Captain Demetrios was tortured into confessing that he beached his ship. Actually, he was asleep when someone turned the ship into the shore where robbers were waiting. When Demetrios woke and went to investigate, he was hit on the head and lost consciousness. He was not the perpetrator or an accomplice in these terrible crimes of robbery and the indiscriminate murder of crew and passengers who got in the way of the robbers."

"Casca, the allegation that the confession was extracted by torture has been made in court, but the answer is that the confession was corroborated. Demetrios confessed to details of the crime that he couldn't have known if he was asleep or unconscious. What do you say about that?"

"We say that the so-called corroboration is phony. While being tortured Demetrios denied any part in the robbery. He stuck to his story. He didn't know what happened. But then he was made aware of the answer wanted by the judge's assessor. The assessor told him, for instance, that he knew it was Demetrios who turned the ship into the shore. When he again denied it, they tortured him even more harshly until he could no longer stand the pain and screamed, yes he was the one who turned the ship into the shore."

"But the interrogation was held in the presence of a Roman judge, Judge Sulpicius, who surely knows the Rescript of Trajan regarding questioning under torture. Magistrates should not ask leading questions during torture. Are you saying Judge Sulpicius violated his duty?"

"He did not himself ask leading questions, but his assessor did, in the judge's presence. He just looked the other way."

"I find that hard to believe. Why would Judge Sulpicius act in that way?"

"I don't know. I can't say. All I know is what Captain Demetrios tells me. And I believe him, not just because he is my client, but because I know in my heart he is telling the truth."

"Have you talked with anyone present at the interrogation besides the victim. The *carnifex* torturer, perhaps, or the lictors?"

"We tried to talk with the *carnifex* and the lictors. They all denied there was any irregularity, but not very convincingly. A lot of hemming and hawing, and eyes shifting away. It was a *pro forma* denial."

"I will talk to Judge Sulpicius. Now, what else do you have for me?"

"Just that the confession doesn't hold up. There is no corroboration. And since there is no other evidence against Captain Demetrios, the prosecution's burden of proof has not been met. Therefore, the Captain should have been acquitted at the trial and he should be acquitted on the appeal."

Severus nodded his head in acknowledgement. "A good legal argument, Casca, but perhaps I should talk to the defendant Demetios to hear what he actually says."

"It will do you no good, *eminentissime*. Not just his body, but his mind has been seriously damaged by the torture. He twitches, he babbles, he makes little sense now.

Severus closed his eyes and took a deep breath. There was silence for a long moment. Then he turned to Opimius. "You have a personal interest in seeing the Captain acquitted, don't you?"

"Indeed, I do, *eminentissime*. Right now, I have not only lost my ship, but I might be liable for damages to Antipater and to all the investors for loss of the cargo. It is almost a sidelight that I too was an investor in the cargo to the tune of a million sesterces. In short, if the voyage had been successful, I would have reaped a large profit. As of now, however, I am ruined. So, yes, I do have a personal interest in seeing Captain Demetrios acquitted."

"And I might add," immediately interposed the lawyer in his mellifluous voice, "that my client's personal interest does not affect what happened here. It is the goddess Justitia herself who calls out for vindication. Whatever my client's interest, Captain Demetrios is innocent."

"By the way, Opimius, I am told that both the *Andromeda*'s Shipmaster Scylax and the First Mate, Baaldo, had previously worked on your ships."

"Yes, they did. And I ended up not liking them. When I learned that Antipater had hired both Scylax and Baaldo for the voyage, that's when I appointed Demetrios as the Captain of the *Andromeda*. I didn't want either Scylax or Baaldo as Captain."

"I am also told, Opimius, that you and Antipater don't care much for each other."

"Yes. That's true. To put it bluntly, I hate him and he hates me. We have a business rivalry and a personal one."

"Why then did you lease the *Andromeda* to him? Why did you invest in his cargo of silk?"

"I may dislike Antipater, even hate him. But I recognize he is a superior business man and I stood to make a lot of money if he had a successful voyage with the *Andromeda*. That's why I made my ship available to him and why I invested in his cargo. As it happened, though, I've lost out enormously."

"Thank you both," concluded Severus. "I will pursue the matter to the satisfaction of the goddess Justitia."

"We can ask for no more," concluded the lawyer, and the meeting ended.

When both visitors had gone, Severus called in his court clerk. "Quintus, send a message to Judge Sulpicius. Tell him I would like to see him. I have a few questions about the Demetrios case that he might know the answers to."

Proculus wrote out a message on a waxed tablet and had one of the court slaves take it to Judge Sulpicius' chambers in the colonnade on the other side of the Temple of Mars the Avenger.

It was only a few minutes later that Severus received a reply inviting him to come over right now, if that was convenient for him. It was. And Severus immediately headed across the forum.

XIII

JUDGE SEVERUS TALKS WITH JUDGE SULPICIUS

Judge Severus was greeted at the entrance to Judge Sulpicius' chambers by Judge Sulpicius himself and, after exchanging greeting kisses, was escorted inside, where fruit and wine were already set out on a table. Judge Sulpicius sat on one side of the table, while Severus was motioned to sit on the other.

Judge Sulpicius was a thin man, not quite as tall as Severus, and had the same rather imperious, almost arrogant, look about him that he had when he sat on the Tribunal. But while appearing stand-offish and superior, he put on a friendly show for a colleague.

"How nice it is to see you, Judge Severus. I hope this new *cognitio* of yours will not interfere too much with your retirement."

"I hope not, but to some degree, of course, it must. Nevertheless, it is a paradox, perhaps, that I should enjoy the tranquility of retirement, while missing the action of a criminal case, while I enjoy the action of a criminal case while missing the tranquility of retirement."

"When I retire, I hope I will welcome that paradox. For too many of our colleagues, retirement is languishing."

"They then should read Seneca on retirement. His embracing of liberal studies points the way to a fruitful retirement, in pursuit of learning and wisdom, with or without paradoxes."

"Seneca is a trustworthy guide in philosophy, even though a hypocrite in practice. But tell me, Judge Severus, what did you want to see me about?" With his question, judge Sulpicius' demeanor became slightly defensive.

"I will get straight to the point, Judge Sulpicius. As you must know, I have been appointed by the Urban Prefect to investigate the case of Demetrios, the Captain of the merchant ship *Andromeda*. You convicted him of wrecking the ship, of being a conspirator and accomplice to robbery and murder and sentenced him to death in the arena. The case is now on appeal to the Urban Prefect."

Sulpicius nodded, indicating Severus should go on.

"I will be blunt. In the course of my investigation, I have now encountered claims from two sources that Demetrios' confession, obtained under judicial torture, was flawed in that the answers your assessor wanted were supplied to him before more torture was applied. Therefore, there was no actual corroboration."

Judge Sulpicius answered immediately and with some force. "I ordered Demetrios subjected to judicial torture, that is true. And I understand, as the Emperor Trajan ruled, that evidence from torture is considered weak and dangerous, but is not to be rejected entirely. I am also aware of the Rescript of Antoninus Pius that torture is to be used only where truth cannot be obtained in any other way. I considered this to be just that situation."

"It is not so much the judicial order of torture that worries me," replied Severus, "but the accusations that the requirement of asking only direct questions was not observed. Specifically, it has been alleged that your assessor, in your presence, told Demetrios the answers he wanted to hear, and then only when more drastic torture was applied, did Demetrios give those answers. And then those answers were regarded as the corroboration needed for crediting a confession extracted by torture."

"I don't know your sources, Judge Severus. But those accusations are lies, perhaps spread by those who want Demetrios acquitted. You must know that the civil case for damages for loss of the ship and the cargo of silks depends on the outcome of the criminal case, on who is found guilty of the crimes. If Captain Demetrios, who was appointed by the owners of the *Andromeda*, is guilty, then the owners of the ship cannot collect damages for its loss. Indeed, they might have to pay damages to the charterer for loss of the cargo. On the other hand, if the Captain is innocent, then the charterer must bear the costs for the losses of ship and cargo. A great deal of money, millions of sesterces, depends on the verdict. Both sides therefore have strong motives to either convict or acquit

Demetrios. Accordingly, each side structures its legal case and spreads self-serving rumors to further its interests.

"I, on the other hand, am a Roman judge with no interest one way or the other in the outcome, except as dictated by the goddess Justitia. So I conducted the interrogation under torture following all the rules. Demetrios' confession was extracted under torture, but it was corroborated by his relating facts of the crime he couldn't have know if he had been unconscious, as he alleges. I did not look the other way while my assessor asked leading questions. That did not happen.

"So Judge Severus, I trust I have put your concerns to rest. The accusations against me are false. Nothing more than familiar Roman *vituperatio*, this time bolstered by huge financial interests in the outcome of the case."

Sulpicius thought for a moment. "Perhaps I should bring my assessor in to tell you what happened. After all, he is the one accused of feeding answers."

"That's a good idea. I would like to hear his account."

Sulpicius got up and went into the anteroom and quickly returned followed by a young man.

"Judge Severus, this is Junius Catius Asper, my assessor. He's fresh out of law school."

"It's a pleasure to meet you, Judge Severus," said Asper, sitting down next to Judge Sulpicius. He was a handsome young man, though somewhat smug in his manner. "All law students are great admirers of you and your crime solving. You are becoming a legend in the law schools."

"I didn't know that. I'm honored. What law school did you go to? Are you a Proculean or a Sabinian?"

"I went to the law school of Proculus. Did you go there too, Judge Severus?"

"No. I went to the law school of Sabinus and Cassius, as did my father and his father. So I'm a Sabinian."

"I'm also a Proculean," chimed in Judge Sulpicius. "And that's another reason why I am a stickler for the law. We Proculeans are noted for our adherence to the old, traditional, conservative forms, while you Sabinians are the ones who believe in getting rid of old forms which you call outdated and no longer suitable."

"We think of ourselves as being more progressive, it's true," countered Severus. "And I would add that I for one favor modern revision or abandonment of outdated legal formulas. Times change and laws must change with them."

"We know that times change," responded Sulpicius. "But we believe in sticking to the original formulas, which are time tested."

Severus addressed the assessor. "Asper, tell me about the questioning of Captain Demetrios while he was being tortured. What kind of questions did you ask him?"

"I asked him only direct questions. I never suggested any answers. Like a good Proculean, I am a stickler for the law. So I followed it."

"There's a rumor going around that you fed answers to Demetrios while he was being tortured."

"Not true. Not true at all. He confessed to facts that he couldn't have known if he was asleep and unconscious, as he alleged. That is good corroboration."

"What were those facts?"

"Facts connected to the steering of the ship onto land, for instance. He confessed he personally handled the tiller. Then he knew facts relating to the robbery, such as torches being used for lighting, and what was stolen. Everything. He knew everything."

"Did he tell you any fact you didn't know before his interrogation?"

Asper stopped to think. "I can't put my finger on one at the moment. But we didn't know everything. He did."

Severus rose. "Thank you, Asper. Thank you, judge."

Severus left in something of a quandary. Judge Sulpicius was persuasive, even convincing. As was his assessor. And Judge Sulpicius was doubly credible because he had no interest in the case other than the pursuit of justice.

But on the other hand, the accusation, according to Vulso, came from one of Judge Sulpicius' lictors who witnessed the judicial torture. The lictor was a credible source too. He would be neutral; he would have no financial interest in the matter. The fact that the lictor later denied any impropriety when questioned by Demetrios' lawyer was not decisive. He might just be avoiding reprisals against himself.

Therefore, thought Severus as he walked across the forum back to his own chambers, he would provisionally believe what Judge Sulpicius and his assessor told him. But it was also necessary to seek out that lictor and perhaps even the torturer and question them. Was the hearsay Vulso heard true? If so, the judge and his assessor were lying. If the judge was telling the truth, then the hearsay accusation was false. But which one was it? The presumption in Roman law would be to credit the judge. As a member of the Equestrian Order, he was an *honestior*, presumed by law to be more credible and entitled to be believed more than an *humilior* lictor, a person of the lower classes.

But Severus knew very well that that presumption was a legal fiction serving the interests of the nobility in Roman society.

And he was after the truth, not fiction.

XIV

ARTEMISIA RETURNS TO THE DRESS SHOP WITH JUDGE SEVERUS, AND VULSO CONFRONTS A SILK TAILOR AND ARRESTS A ROBBER

Artemisia arrived at Vespilla's dress shop at the 5th hour of the morning, accompanied by Judge Severus and Vulso. The judge was dressed in his magistrate's red-purple bordered toga, and Vulso in full centurion's uniform, with the crest on his helmet going from side to side, rather than front to back.

To complete an intimidating impression, the judge and his wife arrived in an 8-bearer official litter of the court of the Urban Prefect. Vulso marched alongside.

One of the shop slaves saw the litter and the Centurion coming and quickly notified Vespilla, who dashed outside. At first sight, she didn't like the looks of it and was already nervous when Severus and Artemisia got out of the litter. Vespilla recognized

'Elektra' and spoke to her, "Elektra, how nice to see you again. But what is this about?"

"This is my husband, Marcus Flavius Severus, *iudex selectus* investigating the *Andromeda* affair. Is there some place we can talk privately?"

Vespilla noticed 'Elektra' spoke Latin with only the hint of an Athenian accent, not the thick heavy one she had a few days before.

"My name is really Artemisia," she said to Vespilla in a calm, friendly voice. "We are not here to cause you any trouble. We just want some information."

Vespilla led them into a back room with a table and chairs.

Judge Severus then took over the conversation. "Vespilla, we know you are an honest woman and run an honest shop. So we mean you no harm. But we also know that silk stolen from the shipwreck of the *Andromeda* is coming onto the market in Rome and we believe that the silk being made into a *stola* for my wife may be from that robbery. We want to know who is selling you the silk." Severus stopped and waited.

Vespilla was silent, thinking something over. She decided to be forthright.

"*Eminentissime*, I did not know that the silk for Elektra's dress is stolen silk. So I will tell you the silk for your wife is being made into a *stola* by a tailor named Glaukos. He makes clothes and sells them, for my shop and other shops as well. His shop is on the Quirinal Hill on the street *Alta Semita*, just across from the Altar of Nero. Please don't tell him I told you about him."

"Thank you Vespilla. I appreciate your help. We will not need to bother you again."

Severus, Artemisia and Vulso then got up to leave. Artemisia stopped to tell Vespilla that her customer Valeria did not know of her impersonation. It was a lie intended to keep Valeria in the good graces of Vespilla. Of course, Vespilla would have to believe the lie, which she probably wouldn't, or forget about it to keep Valeria as a customer, which she probably would.

Leaving the dress shop, Severus and Artemisia went back to the Forum of Augustus, while Vulso collected four soldiers of the Urban Cohort and went to the tailor Glaukos' shop on the *Alta Semita*.

Vulso had no trouble finding the shop and strode in with two of the soldiers, while two others stood guard outside. He saw a workshop with a number of men and women at tables engrossed in sewing clothes. Everyone looked up when the soldiers entered.

"Which one is Glaukos?" asked Vulso directly.

"I am," answered an old man with wispy white hair who came up to Vulso. "What's going on? What's this about?" He was nervous and jumpy.

"You and everybody on the premises are under arrest." He turned to Glaukos. "Where are the silks?"

"What silks? I have only…"

Vulso slapped him in the face. "Don't mess with me. I know you have silks stolen from the ship *Andromeda*." He turned to the soldiers with him. "Search the place. Tear it apart." He turned back to Glaukos. "Either give up the silks or we will tear this place to shreds and subject you and all the workers to judicial torture until we find what we're looking for. Is that what you want?"

Glaukos was now trembling.

"Give him what he wants," said an old woman who rushed forward from one of sewing tables. "I'm Glaukos' wife. We recently received a new batch of raw silks from *Seres*, but we didn't know they were stolen. I'll show you where they are."

Vulso told the soldiers to hold off and followed Glaukos' wife who led him into a storage room in back. She pointed to several bales. "There are three bales of silk. That's all we could afford at the moment."

"Who did you get them from?"

"Not from our usual supplier of fabric for clothes. But from someone who said he knew of our tailoring and offered us *serica* at a good price. So we bought some."

"Is it real *serica* from *Seres*?"

"It's real all right. It's the finest I've ever seen."

"Who sold it to you?"

"I don't know who he is. But he said he'd be back on the Ides, that's tomorrow, to see if we wanted more silk. He said his name was Felix."

Vulso left the shop wondering if this might be the same Felix who recruited Hector and others from the streets to unload cargo. Felix was a common name, but Vulso made a bet with himself that it was the same Felix. In any case, he would find out tomorrow.

The next day Vulso and his soldiers were in the back of the Glaukos tailor shop waiting for Felix to show up. They had arrived an hour before the shop opened for business at the 2nd hour and were let in and hidden in the back by Glaukos.

They didn't have long to wait. Two hours later, Glaukos' wife came into the back and in a low voice told Vulso. "He's here."

Vulso, followed by his men, left the back room and went directly to the front of the shop where a large man with a short military beard was talking to Glaukos.

"Are you Felix?" asked Vulso as the man noticed him approaching.

"Yes. And who are you?"

Vulso replied, "I am a Centurion in the Urban Cohort and an aide to Judge Marcus Flavius Severus, who is investigating the theft of silk from the ship *Andromeda*. I know that you are selling silk from that theft."

"I don't know who told you...." Felix' reply was cut short by a hard slap to his face. Felix wobbled at his knees.

"Stand up straight," said Vulso.

Felix stood up straight, grimacing and rubbing his cheek.

"You are now under arrest." Two of the soldiers pulled Felix' hands behind his back, handcuffed him and pushed him out of the store. "I'll go ahead to Judge Severus' chambers," Vulso told one of the soldiers. You bring him along. Don't talk to him or tell him anything. We will deal with him there."

Vulso accosted Felix. "We're taking you to the *iudex selectus* investigating the *Andromeda* affair. If you cooperate, you will receive leniency. If not, you will be tortured and killed horribly. Think it over on the way to court."

Felix stared at Vulso defiantly. But as he saw Vulso's return look of defiance along with a sinister looking smile, Felix looked away. Then Vulso left.

An hour later, Felix sat in a chair across the table from Judge Severus. Vulso sat next to Felix. The prisoner's handcuffs had been removed and he was offered wine to drink and a bowl of fruit to eat. He nervously gobbled the fruit and sloshed down the wine without tasting either.

"Now Felix," began Judge Severus, mildly, "I hope you understand the position you are in. We know that you recruited people off the street to unload silk from the shipwrecked *Andromeda*. We know that you took them to an *insula* in the Subura to be interviewed by the Whale. Some of these recruits of yours have been captured and will identify you. We also know that you sold some of the silks to the tailoring establishment of Glaukos.

"Now I want to know where the stolen silks are, how you got them and who else you sold them to."

Felix looked frightened.

"They'll kill me if I tell."

"I'll sentence you to death if you don't tell. And you are in my custody now, not theirs. So you'll tell me everything, won't you?"

Felix closed his eyes and hung his head. "If I tell you, what then? Will you kill me even if I tell?"

"No, Felix. I won't. You'll be punished for your part in the crime, that's certain, but you'll live."

"Will you sentence me *ad metallum*, to the mines? I don't want to go there. It's worse than death there."

"I will not bargain with you about the sentence, though I promise it will not be death if you cooperate satisfactorily. I'll decide the sentence when I hear what you have to say and when I decide how truthful and helpful you've been. Make up your mind. I want answers now."

Felix took a deep breath and audibly exhaled.

"The silks are kept in a warehouse, in the Horrea Lolliana, by the Tiber near Mount Testaceus. They're under the name of Balaena, the Whale. That's where I go to pick up bales I sell and deliver to customers. Whale tells me when to go, how many bales to take and who to take them to."

Severus nodded at Vulso who knew how to interpret the nod. He immediately went into the anteroom and nodded to Crantor who was seated there. The pankratiast bodyguard replaced Vulso and sat down next to Felix. Then Vulso dictated a message to Proculus to be immediately sent to headquarters of the Urban Cohort in the Castra Praetoria. It told them to quickly organize two *contubernia* of soldiers and meet Vulso in two hours at the warehouse of Lolliana by the Tiber. They were to bring a wheeled vehicle sufficiently roomy to carry away a large supply of stolen silk.

Then Proculus prepared a court order for invasion of the warehouse, and gave it to Severus, who signed it. Proculus gave it to Vulso, who then headed out of the forum in the direction of the warehouse Lolliana to scout out the area ahead of the arrival of his troops.

Meanwhile, Severus continued to question Felix, who continued to spill information about organizing a band of people to unload the silks from the *Andromeda*. Felix alleged that he took no part in killing anyone at the ship; he only oversaw the 'stevedores' unloading the cargo. He only learned of the place and time of the operation from the Whale and carried out any and all of his tasks at Whale's direction. Whale resided in the *insula* and rarely went outside because of his huge size.

"As far as I know, he only goes out to meet with someone who gives him orders."

"With *Ipse*?"

"Yes, with *Ipse*. But I never met *Ipse*. Only the Whale knows who he is."

"I also want to know where Scylax, the Shipmaster of the *Andromeda* and the First Mate Baaldo are."

"I don't know where they are."

"They live in your *insula,* don't they? The *Insula Octavia*."

"They did before the robbery. Now they are somewhere else, but only the Whale knows where."

"But they're alive, aren't they?"

"Oh yes. They're alive and living it up, I understand. Sometimes they even come to the *insula* to confer with the Whale. But they live somewhere else now."

"By the way," said Severus. "The apartment building is called the *Insula Octavia*. Is there an actual person named Octavia in charge? Or is it just a name?"

"Yes. There is an Octavia. I met her – once. I think she owns the building and collects rents from the Whale. She's never talked to me, though"

"Tell me what you know about her. What does she look like? Where does she live?"

"She's a young woman, very good looking, well dressed. I think she inherited the building and changed its name to hers. I don't know where she lives or what her status in society is or anything else about her. You'll have to ask the Whale."

When Severus had finished questioning Felix, court slaves took him to a prison where he would be kept on hand for further questioning and to await trial. Meanwhile, Straton had come into the judge's chambers.

Severus addressed Straton and Crantor. "I'm worried. When Felix doesn't return to the *insula*, they'll become suspicious that something happened to him. Maybe they already are. If we want to arrest the Whale, we had better go to the *insula* now. Straton, how fast can we organize a raid?"

"It would take a while to put together a proper raid. So I would suggest that we three hurry up to the *Insula Octavia* while sending a message to the *Vigiles* to meet us there. There's a station of Cohort II of the *Vigiles* near the Clivus Suburanus, not far from the *insula*."

Severus called his court clerk back in. "Quintus, send a court slave immediately running to the station of Cohort II of the *Vigiles* near the Clivus Suburanus. I want at least one *contubernium* of *Vigiles* to meet us at the *Insula Octavia* as fast as possible. If they get there ahead of us, they should not let anyone leave the *insula*."

Then Severus, Straton and Crantor headed out of the rear of the Forum of Augustus and into the

Subura at a brisk pace. "Evidently," said the judge, "the plot to beach *Andromeda* and rob it was organized by the Whale from the *Insula Octavia*. Now we will go to the *Insula Octavia* to beach the Whale."

XV

VULSO RAIDS A WAREHOUSE

Vulso arrived at the Warehouse Lolliana before any of the Urban Cohort soldiers. The warehouse was situated at the docks a short distance downriver from the main warehouse area with the gigantic Warehouse Galbana behind the Porticus Aemilia. Vulso saw what looked like ordinary activity going on, people putting merchandise into the warehouse and taking merchandise out. But since it was the late afternoon, things were winding down. He saw nothing like bales of silk being removed.

He went immediately to the office of clerks, bypassing without reading the placard by the entrance giving the services and rules of the warehouse. A small, old man in an ordinary brown tunic was behind a counter. Seeing Vulso's centurion's helmet, he eagerly offered to help.

"Are you the custodian of the warehouse?"

"I'm Gaius Erucianus, his assistant. The custodian has already left for the day."

Vulso produced the court order signed by Judge Severus. "This is a court order allowing a search of the storage area rented by Balaena, the Whale. Troops of the Urban Cohort are on their way to join me in the search. Has anyone been here today to remove items from Balaena's storage area?"

"No, not that I know of. But let me check the registration book." Erucianus went to a large bound codex on the counter and consulted the last few pages. "No. No removals are recorded for today. The last removal was done by an authorized agent of Balaena by the name of Felix and that was three days ago. Of course, I don't know what was removed."

About a half hour later, troops of the Urban Cohort arrived with vehicles for carrying away whatever they found.

"Take us to Balaena's storage area," said Vulso to the custodian, who led them into the back to a large set of padlocked doors. "I don't have a key," said Erucianus.

"Open the door," said Vulso to one of the troops who carried a large metal cutter. The soldier proceeded to snap the padlock in half and remove it from the hasp. Two other soldiers pushed open the doors, while another lit a torch and they all entered the room.

"Eheu!" exclaimed one of the soldiers. "Lots of stuff in here."

Vulso looked around. Occupying most of the room were bales and bales of fabric piled one atop another. Each of the bales had labels dangling from the top with the letters 'SRC'.

"What does SRC stand for?" asked one of the soldiers.

"My guess," replied Vulso, "is *serica*. But we'll make sure. Soldier, open the top bale."

The soldier unsheathed his legionary knife, cut off labels and opened bales. Another came forward with a torch and a third told Vulso that he was sent here because he knew about linens and silks and other valuable cloth. The contents of some of the bales were in the form of fabric rolls and some in bundles of threads, just like the examples Artemisia had shown them at their conference in the judge's chambers. The fabric expert proceeded to examine the fabric rolls and the bundles of threads. "It's *serica*, all right. No doubt about it."

"Impound it," said Vulso. "Take it to the vehicles outside, but leave a few bales here. We'll use them as bait."

Soldiers began to remove the bales of silk and put them in the waiting vehicles. Vulso turned to the custodian. "We will leave a few soldiers here dressed as clerks. You will have one with you at all times. Some others will be around also dressed as clerks. Anyone seeking access to the Balaena storage area will be arrested. You will inform the chief custodian when he comes in."

The custodian gave a big smile. He had already figured out that the bales must be from the sensational case of the shipwrecked *Andromeda*. He couldn't wait to tell not only the chief custodian, but all his friends, his family and everyone else he ran into.

XVI

THE INSULA OCTAVIA
AND THE WHALE

While Vulso was discovering the stolen bales of silk, Judge Severus, Crantor and Straton arrived at the *Insula Octavia*. Simultaneously, a *contubernium* of eight police of the *Vigiles* came on the street. One of them spotted the magistrate's toga worn by Judge Severus and introduced himself.

"*Eminentissime*, my name is Publius Lollianus. I am a Centurion of the *Vigiles* and command this *contubernium*. How can we help you?"

"We are going to enter the *Insula Octavia*, just down the street. My assistants," he said, pointing to Crantor and Straton, "will come with me to find someone named Balaena, the Whale, and arrest him. Two of your troopers will come with us, while the rest will guard the entrance. People who say they are residents can come in, but no one should be allowed to leave."

And with that, Severus, Crantor and Straton went to the entrance of the *Insula Octavia*. The *ianitor* who had been there in the morning was still there. Only the vat of feces by the entrance had been removed for use as fertilizer, but the doorman was still using his bag of rose petals to ward off the still lingering odor.

Straton accosted him.

"*Salve.* You may remember me from this morning."

The porter looked him over. "Oh yes. But you weren't in uniform then."

"I am now. This is Marcus Flavius Severus, *iudex selectus*, and his every word is to be obeyed without question. Otherwise there will be arrests. Do you understand me?"

The porter nodded.

"Now, tell me where the Whale is."

"I don't know where the Whale is. He left a few hours ago."

"What? Did he just walk away?"

"No. An 8-bearer litter came for him. He went inside the litter and that's the last I saw of him."

"Which way did the litter go?"

"That way," said the *ianitor* pointing. "Toward the Clivus Suburanus, toward the Esquiline Hill."

"Show us his apartment."

The porter led them inside on the first floor, behind the stairs, to a spacious room with a table, a bed, a wash basin and a chest.

"Can you open the chest?" said Severus to Straton, looking at the lock.

Straton took a set of small tools from a leather pouch he wore on his belt, and proceeded to pick the lock, soon opening it without much trouble. They then looked inside. There were clothes, sandals and some rolled up scrolls, which Straton handed to the judge.

"We'll have to read these, whatever they are. Meanwhile, as long as we're here, we might as well conduct a real raid on this *insula*. We want to find out who is here from the crew of the *Andromeda*, and what people know about the Whale, who he is, where he's from, *et cetera*."

"It's getting late, though," said Straton. "We don't have the time and resources at the moment. How will we know who is from the crew, for instance? Suppose, one of the officers is here, how will we know who he is?"

"We can only do that tomorrow morning," replied the judge. "So no one will be allowed to leave until then. The *Vigiles* will see to that.

"And in case ship's officers like Scylax and Baaldo happen to be here, I will send messages and military escorts to bring Antipater, the charterer of *Andromeda*, and Opimius, the owner of *Andromeda*, here first thing tomorrow morning. Their task will be to identify officers or crew from the *Andromeda*."

"Why do we need both of them? Won't Antipater be sufficient?"

"Normally yes. But remember, Antipater probably doesn't want us to find the Shipmaster and First Mate because he doesn't want the conviction of the Captain compromised. So he might not identify them, even if they're here. But Opimius would be sure to point them out. He would want them found because he wants one or both of them to be guilty of beaching the ship, not the Captain he appointed. And *vice versa* for anyone Opimius might not want identified. Antipater would be sure to point them out.

"In any case, I'm going home now, and Straton and Crantor, you can too." He turned to address Lollianus, the *Vigiles* Centurion. "Can you keep everything under control until morning?"

"No problem, *eminentissime*. We'll see no one leaves the *insula*."

"Excellent," replied the judge, and he, accompanied by his bodyguard Crantor, headed off toward his own *insula* on the Caelian Hill.

SCROLL IV

XVII

JUDGE SEVERUS
INTERVIEWS OCTAVIA

Early the next morning, while Flaccus, Vulso and Straton were conducting interviews of the residents at the *Insula Octavia*, Severus had his court clerk Proculus go to the offices of the City Aedile, where records pertaining to ownership of buildings in the City were kept.

There was more than one *Insula Octavia* in the City, the records disclosed, but the one in the Subura was owned by someone named Octavia Prisca. Her address, Proculus reported to the judge, was given as a *domus* on the Caelian Hill, not far from where Severus lived. Her *domus*, curiously, was on same street as the *domus* of Senator Titus Paculus. Severus had just been on that street to talk to him as the former owner of freedmen Antipater and Zeno, the former the charterer of the *Andromeda* and the latter his rival in business and over the Paculus' former concubine Cassandra. Could there possibly be a connection between Titus Paculus and Octavia Prisca? They might know each other if they live in houses on the same street, though in crowded Rome that was not a certainty by any means.

When Octavia Prisca's address had been located, Severus had a message sent to her, saying that he wished to meet with her in her home that morning at the 5th hour. It was a matter of some importance to a legal investigation he was conducting as *iudex selectus*. The court messenger was told to wait for a reply and received one agreeing to the meeting.

Before the 5th hour Severus, with Crantor and Alexander, walked the short distance from his *insula* to Octavia's *domus*. They were met at the entrance by an old man and four young slaves, two boys and two girls. The man introduced himself as the bailiff of the house, invited Severus and his two companions inside, and led them into the atrium, saying that Octavia Prisca would be out shortly.

The atrium was furnished quite elegantly, with tasteful mosaics of sea creatures in blue waters on the floor and finely painted green garden scenes on the walls. While they were all admiring the atrium, two women came in, one in her 30's, the other in her 20's. The older woman was very attractive, the younger stunning. Both wore their dark hair long and were dressed in what looked like fine silk *stolae,* off-white with pale blue hems. Both wore blue lapis lazuli necklaces. Both dresses modestly reached to the ankles, but immodestly were made of see-through silk, barely concealing anything.

Severus controlled his facial expression, appreciating their allure though thinking that it was imprudent, even impertinent, that they would wear such revealing clothes before a Roman judge present in his official capacity. His two companions reacted differently. Alexander blushed. Crantor licked his lips.

"I am Octavia," said the older woman. "This is my private secretary, Persephone. Please come into the *tablinum*."

Severus introduced Alexander as his private secretary and Crantor as his bodyguard, and they followed the women into the room behind the atrium. There was a table holding fruit and wine in elegant transparent glass bowl and cups. Octavia and Persephone sat on one side, while the three men took chairs set up for them on the other side.

"What can I do for you, *eminentissime*?" said Octavia, in a mild business-like but nevertheless alluring voice.

Severus drank some wine.

"As *iudex selectus*, I am investigating the *Andromeda* affair. In the course of my investigation, I found that several people connected with the case live in the *Insula Octavia*, the Subura apartment building you own."

Octavia nodded.

"Please tell me first, when and how you came to own this *insula*?"

"I inherited it four years ago from my husband. He died of the plague that struck the City. I'm sure you remember that disaster."

"I certainly do," replied Severus. "Fortunately, I along with my whole *familia* left Rome and stayed in Athens for a year until we heard the plague had dissipated in the Urbs."

"Like most people, we stayed in the City. Why not? Since plagues are caused by the anger of the gods, we prayed to the gods and invoked magic spells to appease them. *Abraxus, abraxus*, we kept on repeating these magic words and others all through the day. We all wore magic charms as well. We wrote magic spells on our door frames. We tried everything that was supposed to help. We drank vinegar and ate mustard. We couldn't get earth from Armenia or milk from Stabiae, but we drank urine from young boys. None of it did any good. And the doctors, of course, were useless. And it was not only my husband who died in the plague, but I also lost a sister and many friends. So I'm curious, judge, why were you smart enough to leave rather than stay?"

"My wife and I both believe Hippocrates and Galen are right about the causes of disease and sickness and plagues. They are not caused by gods or demons, but by imbalances, either within the humors inside the human body or by the environment, by pollution in the air. Miasma, it's called. And since it wasn't inner imbalances of humors that affected so many different people the same way all at once, it must have been miasma in the air. So, just as we isolate lepers, we thought of a city full of diseased people almost as a leper colony and went to Athens, where my wife is from and where her family lives. Fortunately, the co-Emperor Lucius Verus, who was alive at the time, entrusted me with a mission to Athens, so that made it certain the whole *familia* would leave plague-ridden Rome."

"Looking back, of course, that's what we should have done. My husband had a horrible death as did others stricken, breaking out in pustules, having uncontrollable diarrhea, becoming delirious, burning up with fever. But at least I survived, though many family and friends died."

Octavia's voice broke, overcome by tragic memories. Then, at the point of tears, she got hold of herself and returned to the topic at hand, but talk of the plague turned her see-through dress from alluring to incongruous.

"In any case," she continued, wiping her eyes with a handkerchief, "my husband left me well-endowed. He owned several *insulae* in the City, three in the Subura, one on the Esquiline Hill and another here on the Caelian Hill. I own all of them now."

"Do you know the residents of your apartment houses?"

"Not really. No. I have my freedmen make the rounds to collect rents. Occasionally, I might visit one or the other *insula* to see that it is in good condition and everything is running as it's supposed to."

"When did you last visit the *Insula Octavia* in the Subura?"

"Perhaps several months ago. I don't really remember."

"When you went there, who did you talk to?"

"The person in charge of that insula is named *Balaena*. The Whale. He is very, very fat, but very competent as a manager of the *insula*. I spoke to him."

"Do you know where the Whale is now?"

"Isn't he where he always is? In his room on the first floor of the *insula*?"

"No. He is not there now. Do you know Felix, who also lives there?"

"I believe I met him once."

"And the sailors Scylax and Baaldo? Do you know them?"

"I don't believe so. Are they residents? I don't know all the people in the building, as I've said. But why are you asking about these people?"

"Scylax and Baaldo were officers of the ship-wrecked vessel *Andromeda*. Felix employed people as stevedores to unload the *Andromeda* of its silks. Then we caught him selling silks stolen from the *Andromeda*. The Whale, we're told, directed it all, interviewing the stevedores and directing the activities of Felix. When we captured Felix, the Whale left your *insula*, hurriedly, in a litter. We are searching for him now."

"I'm shocked. I can hardly believe it. The Whale and Felix involved in the *Andromeda* affair. Residents of my *insula* officers on the ship? Are you sure about all this?"

"Positive."

"I will help you all I can, though I don't know how."

"The Whale may seek to contact you. If he does, I expect you will let me know."

"Of course."

"By the way, I was on this street just the other day, talking to Senator Titus Paculus. He lives just down the street. Do you know him by any chance?"

"Titus? Of course I know him. He's my cousin."

"Do you know that his freedman Antipater was the charterer of the *Andromeda*?"

"Yes, I knew that. I know Antipater too. A money-mad scoundrel. A hustler. Totally untrustworthy. It doesn't surprise me at all that *he* would be involved in something as questionable as the *Andromeda* affair."

Severus rose to conclude the interview. Octavia rose and escorted Severus back into the atrium. While she talked to him, her young private secretary Persephone motioned Alexander aside and asked him whether, as Judge Severus' private secretary, he could take dictation in Tironian Notes shorthand.

"Yes, I can," replied Alexander, his face turning slightly red in the close presence of Persephone's perfume and pulchritude.

"I'm learning it myself. I think it's fascinating. Cicero's secretary Tiro must have been very clever to invent it. But I have to tell you, Alexander, that I'm dissatisfied with my teacher. Do you teach it at all? I would love to learn from you." She said it in such a way that Alexander became almost tongue-tied, especially when she emphasized the word 'love'.

"I d, d, don't know. I'll have to ask the judge. I do get time to myself, maybe I could t' t' t' teach you then."

"I really hope you can." She gave him a warm, winning smile and pressed his hand in hers.

On the way back to Severus' apartment, Alexander reported his conversation with Persephone.

"I think it's a set-up," said Crantor. "I don't think Octavia is as unknowing as she makes out. Maybe she wants Persephone to pump Alexander for information about our investigation."

"Maybe Persephone was just taken with Alexander," said Severus. "Alexander, what do you think? What do you want to do?"

Alexander couldn't keep from blushing. "I would like to get to know her, I have to admit. She seems very intelligent and she's very beautiful and she wants to learn shorthand."

"Send Persephone a message that you have some time tomorrow afternoon to begin teaching her Tironian Notes. Crantor may be right that Octavia wants to find out what we know and where we are in the investigation. But I want to find out more about Octavia. I agree with Crantor that Octavia may not be as innocent and unknowing as she makes out. There's was just too much going on in her *insula*. I'm suspicious."

Severus had a thought. "Alexander, when you see Persephone tomorrow, mention to her off-handedly that we're looking for someone named *Ipse*, who we think is the head of the criminal enterprise. And say that her cousin Titus Paculus is one of our suspects."

"Why do you want to do that?" asked Alexander. "Do you have any reason to think Paculus is *Ipse*?"

Severus smiled, mostly to himself, but discernable to Alexander and Crantor. "No. I don't. But let's just see what happens."

XVIII

AN ATTACK IN A PARK

The next morning at the 1ˢᵗ hour, Judge Severus, as he had been doing for the past few days, took his dog Argos for a walk in the nearby *Campus Caelemontanus*, a small park on the Caelian hill. Crantor was with him and they were continuing their running conversation about sports, both Greek and Roman. When they entered the park, Severus unleashed Argos so he could run around freely. Usually there were a few people in the park with their dogs, but at the moment there was no one else in sight, either human or canine. Still Argos ran around happily, chasing squirrels, which he never caught.

"I've always thought," opined Severus to Crantor, "that the javelin throw should be a separate event, and not just part of the pentathlon."

"And do you think the same for the discus and long jump?"

"Yes. I think each one should be a separate event, as well as being part of the pentathlon. Running the *stadion* and wrestling are separate events, as well as being part of the pentathlon, so why shouldn't javelin, discus and long jump also be separate events?"

"I don't know why," replied Crantor, "except history and tradition. That's the way it's always been. Isn't that a good enough reason?"

"Not for an amateur javelin thrower like me. I want to see…"

Severus never finished his thought, because at that moment four men emerged from a copse of trees with swords drawn, heading at a deliberate pace toward Severus.

Crantor held his arm in front of Severus, motioning him to stand back, while he quickly took the stance of a pankratiast, left leg forward and bent, right leg straight and behind, left arm forward with palm facing outward, right arm back with a fist.

The largest swordsman came forward slowly, trying to get to Severus. The judge was behind his bodyguard, who moved to block the path of the swordsman. The other three men, also with drawn swords, were spread out behind the first one.

Suddenly the first swordsman rushed at Crantor with his sword thrust forward. With a quick athletic movement, Crantor blocked the sword arm aside with his left arm, stepped in and punched the assailant right in his face with a blow so devastating that the swords man simply collapsed unconscious, his face all bloody, his sword dropped to the ground.

As a second swordsman came up, Crantor moved faster, again blocking the sword arm to the side, but instead of punching him, twisted him around and held him around the neck in a choke hold from behind, and turned him into a shield facing the other assailants. But the person in Crantor's grip did not submit easily and struggled to escape. Instead of fighting him, Crantor right then and there violently pulled up on the choke hold and broke his neck, killing him.

The other two men didn't like what they were seeing and started to hesitate. But just then Argos, who saw what was going on, and realized his master might be in danger, rushed to the fray and leaped on the back of one of the other assailants, viciously growling and biting him. The human screamed in pain and struggled in vain. He was no match for the big black Molossian hound.

The last assailant then ran away as fast as he could.

Severus walked over to the man Argos was assaulting and commanded his dog to stop, while telling the victim on the ground not to move.

Meanwhile the first assailant who Crantor had knocked unconscious revived.

Severus stood over him. "Who sent you?"

The man looked at Severus defiantly and said nothing.

"Who sent you?" asked Crantor.

The man wiped blood from his face, but said nothing.

Crantor looked at Severus. "Go to where Argos and his victim are and look the other way."

"Why?"

"Just do it, Judge."

Severus walked over to Argos and petted him, praising him. The man on the ground remained prone, eliciting menacing growls from Argos if he dared move.

Severus heard a horrible scream from behind him. Aaaaaah. Then there was some silence and then he heard, "no, not again, please don't, aaaaaaah". Then there was silence again, and then "no, please, aaaaaaaah, stop, I'll tell, I'll tell. Only stop."

Crantor dragged the man over to Severus. The man was holding one hand with the other and wincing in pain.

"Who sent you?" asked Crantor, shoving the man forward.

"It was the Whale. The Whale sent me."

"What for?" asked Crantor.

"To kill the judge."

"Where is the Whale?"

"I don't know, I..."

Crantor seized the hand the man was holding inside his other hand.

"No. No. Please. I'll tell. The Whale is in an *insula* on the Esquiline Hill."

"Where on the Esquiline?"

"I don't know how to describe it, but I can take you there."

Severus continued to question him. "What's your name?"

"Kastor."

"Do you work for the Whale?"

"Yes, I do. Me and him," he pointed to the dead assassin. Then he pointed to the man lying at the feet of Argos. "He worked with Furius, the one who got away."

"Tell me about Furius."

"I never saw him before. The Whale told us his name is Furius and that we were to follow him and do what he told us to do. The Whale armed us with swords and Furius led us to the park, pointed you out, and said we were hired to kill you. So we attacked, because the Whale said we should do what Furius told us, but that rat Furius stayed back and then ran away."

By then, members of the *Vigiles* had entered the park, having been alerted by people who had entered the park, seen what was going on, and rushed to the nearby station of the Vth cohort of *Vigiles*, beckoning them to come.

Severus turned to them. "I am Marcus Flavius Severus, *iudex selectus*, and these people tried to kill me. Take them into custody. This one," he pointed to the man Crantor was holding, "is to be kept aside. When I get a unit of the Urban Cohort together, he will take us to the person who sent him."

The *Vigiles* took both assailants away.

Then Severus leashed Argos, petting and praising him, eliciting animated tail wagging, doggie smiles and a prancing gait with his head held high as they all walked back to Severus' *insula.*

"Crantor, you were magnificent. You saved my life. And you got one of them to spill his guts. How did you do that?"

"I broke his fingers, one after the other, promising to break all ten of them, followed by his wrists, ankles, *et cetera*. He gave in after two broken fingers, and as I was about to break the third."

"You were magnificent," repeated Severus. "Simply magnificent."

"Thank you," replied Crantor modestly. "But they were just street thugs, *grassatores*. And Argos was even better than me."

When they reached Severus' apartment and told everyone what happened, Flavia suggested special treats for Argos, and tasty pieces of meat were brought out and fed to him, which he gobbled up. He also gobbled up praise from everyone who eagerly petted and complimented him as his exploits were being recounted. Argos clearly understood the humans were telling what happened and that he was the hero of the story.

"Our Argos is not only like Odysseus' loyal dog Argos in the Odyssey," said Artemisia, "who waited 20 years for him to return and then recognized him in disguise, but he also confirms Plato's view of dogs as true philosophers." Here Artemisia drew on her deep education in Platonic philosophy. "That's because dogs are friendly to those people they know and unfriendly to those they don't know, who they are ignorant of. And, says Plato, any creature that can distinguish meaningfully between knowledge and ignorance must have a philosophic spirit."

"Here's another treat for our true philosopher," said Quintus, "feeding another tasty piece of meat to Argos.

The true philosopher gobbled it up.

XIX

ALEXANDER AND PERSEPHONE

At the 9th hour that afternoon, Alexander arrived at the *domus* of Octavia Prisca. He had with him a *capsa* of scrolls, some with instructional material and some blank, ready to write on. He also had waxed tablets and styli, and ink and reeds for writing scrolls.

Alexander wore a freshly laundered elegant tunic, blue with a Greek geometric design in red on the hem and sleeve ends. He had also been to the baths earlier that day and looked clean, spiffy and eager.

Persephone received him in the atrium. She looked absolutely gorgeous, in an almost see-through silk *stola* like she had worn the previous day. Only this one had an exciting red border rather than pale blue.

She took Alexander into her room where they sat at a table with empty scrolls, ink and pens, waxed tablets and styli. There was wine and fruit on the table. And a bed against one wall.

"Where should we begin?" Persephone asked, sipping wine.

Alexander was not tongue tied this time, but just naturally shy.

"I thought we might start with a basic overview of Tironian Notes shorthand. Is that all right with you?"

She nodded. "Of course."

Alexander became didactic. "Tironian Notes shorthand was invented about 200 years ago by Cicero's freedman Tiro. With it he recorded Cicero's speeches in the courts and in the Senate. It wasn't the first system of shorthand, but it is perhaps the best and has become the standard.

"There are a few thousand signs. Some of them stand for whole words, like the backwards Greek gamma for the Latin word *et* or an I for *in*, or words that are also common particles, like *sub* or *trans* or *prae* or *ex*. Others stand for parts of words, like a backward C for *con*. Others stand for syllables or even for whole phrases."

Alexander went on to expand on the shorthand system. Persephone paid rapt attention and seemed to learn very rapidly, though it was possible she already knew much of what Alexander was teaching her.

After a lesson lasting about an hour, they both stopped and started drinking the wine.

"You know, Alexander," Persephone said in a forthright and bold manner, "I was taken by you the first time I saw you. I saw your intelligence. I don't meet people with your intellect and knowledge. And I know you were once a slave, now freed, just as I was once a slave, now a freedwoman. That is also a bond between us, beyond the fact that I love your mind."

There was nothing that Alexander wanted to hear more than that. It was his intellectual accomplishments and knowledge that he most took pride in. As Severus often said about him, Alexander was more excited by an interesting fact than most people were by a chariot race. And the fact that Persephone saw that in him excited him as well, though he didn't consider that she might have been briefed on his interests.

Their banter moved from casual compliments to warmer feelings as they drank more wine. It didn't take very long before Persephone began to stroke Alexander, before kissing started, before they removed each other's clothes, before they moved to the bed and made love.

Once, twice. They talked between love making, about themselves, their lives. It wasn't long before Alexander was totally smitten, in love. Not only had Persephone insinuated herself into his mind, but he had never experienced the heights of pleasure her sexual skill had brought him to.

"I love you," said Persephone.

"I love you," thought Alexander, but couldn't bring himself to say it.

And they made love once more.

After a while, they had to rest. Then Persephone said to him, "Your judge, I believe, will think I am playing up to you to find out the state of his investigation. My mistress Octavia will think that you are playing up to me to find out what goes on in her *domus*. I don't care what they may think, Alexander, my love, because I have my own desires and wishes. And what I wish is to get out of this house, to get away from Octavia and to start a new life of my own."

Alexander thought instantly that maybe she should start her new life with him. But he was still too shy to say it.

Persephone told him more. "I don't mind that your judge wants to find out what goes on in this house, so I want to tell you something Octavia didn't tell him that he might want to know."

"No," replied Alexander, "I don't want to do that. I don't want to be a spy. I just want you."

"Thank you, Alexander. I appreciate that. I really do. Nevertheless, your judge asked Octavia if she knew Titus Paculus, whose freedman Antipater chartered the *Andromeda*. Octavia said that Paculus was her cousin, as he is. But what she didn't mention is that he is also her lover. She is his mistress. Your judge should know that."

"Thank you for your confidence, Persephone. I trust you all the more." Alexander thought that he should tell her what Judge Severus had wanted him to tell her. It would be an exchange of confidences, something that Alexander wanted to do.

"Persephone, I want you to know something about our investigation."

Persephone looked at him eagerly. "What is it, my love?"

"The judge is looking for someone who is the master criminal, who is really behind the beaching and robbery of *Andromeda*. *Ipse*, 'Himself', he is called.

My judge suspects Titus Paculus, your mistress' cousin, might be *Ipse*."

"Thank you for your confidence, Alexander. Now I trust you all the more."

"You said before, Persephone, that you wanted to get out of this house. Why? Don't you like Octavia?"

"Not particularly, though she doesn't mistreat me and she once saved my life."

"What happened?"

"It had to do with Antipater. Senator Paculus' freedman. I was once with Octavia at her lover's house and Antipater happened to be there too. He saw me and wanted to buy me, then and there. I was a slave at the time. Octavia refused to sell me. Antipater offered a lot of money. She again refused. He then got angry and said he would find a way to buy me. Octavia became incensed and stubborn, as she often is, and told him he never would have me. And then she prevented that from ever happening."

"How?"

"She freed me. Legally I was too young to be manumitted, but she contrived a way. She knows people. Once I was freed, of course, I could no longer be bought. And there is no way I would ever consent to become Antipater's lover."

"That was clever of her. So you must be grateful to Octavia."

"Yes. I am. But I still want a life of my own."

Then they embraced and made love once more, Alexander with his eyes closed, Persephone with hers wide open.

XX

THE WHALE IS FOUND

When Severus arrived at his chambers that morning, Vulso and Straton were there waiting for him, ready to report on their investigation of the residents of the *Insula Octavia* the day before.

Severus reported first, detailing the attack on him that morning. He concluded by telling Vulso to send a message to Urban Cohort headquarters, organizing a raiding party as soon as possible. The Whale was in an *insula* on the Esquiline Hill and the captured assassin, Kastor, would lead them to him.

Vulso went into the anteroom and dictated a message to Proculus to be taken to the Urban Cohort headquarters in the Castra Praetoria. Then he returned and reported to Severus about what they had learned at the *Insula Octavia*.

"What did we learn?" asked Vulso rhetorically. "Not much. We did learn that the *Andromeda*'s officers, Scylax and Baaldo are alive and well, possibly somewhere in the Subura. But no could or would tell us where they are. We'll have to think of some other way to get at them."

"Maybe once we arrest the Whale, we can get him to talk," commented Severus. "He probably knows where they are and a lot more about this crime. He seems to be at its head, except for *Ipse*. Anything else?"

"No. Most of the residents of the *Insula Octavia* had nothing to do with the *Andromeda*. However, there were three crewmen from the ship living there, aside from the missing officers. They seemed forthright in describing what they knew about what happened when the ship was beached and robbed. One of them said he heard the voice of someone he thought was the First Mate Baaldo ordering the crew not to interfere with the unloading of cargo. Then, when he saw robbers with torches attacking the ship, he ran into the night and hid until the robbery was over. Then he walked all the way to Rome and his *insula*."

A few hours later, Severus, Vulso, Crantor and Straton, along with two *contubernia* of the Urban Cohort went up the Esquiline hill to find and arrest the Whale. The captured assassin Kastor led the way, his hand with the broken fingers wrapped in a bandage. He led them first along the *Via Merulana*, then onto a side street and then turned right onto another side street.

"There it is," said Kastor, pointing to a 4-story *insula* at the corner of an intersection. "Yesterday, he was in a room on the first floor, in the back."

Severus and Vulso first sauntered along the street in front of the insula entrance. They saw above the door a painted sign, saying "*Insula Prisca.*"

Severus remembered that Octavia's full name was Octavia Prisca. Her *insula* in the Subura was called the *Insula Octavia*. Probably, then, this *Insula Prisca* also belonged to her.

Severus turned to Vulso. "How should we handle this?"

"Let me go in first. Crantor, Straton, you should come in with me. We'll grab the doorman and order him to take us to the Whale. Everyone else should block off the building. When I have the Whale under arrest, judge, one of us will come back out and get you. You can question him right then and there."

"Go to it," agreed Severus.

Vulso, Crantor and Straton then quickly entered the *insula*, the rest of the troops following behind. Vulso grabbed the doorman, who was taken by surprise, and pushed him toward the back. "Take me to the Whale," ordered Vulso.

The *ianitor* didn't protest at all. Actually, he had a big smile on his face and eagerly motioned Vulso and the other two to follow him. "My name is Ninnius, I am pleased to help the authorities." He led them to the back of the *insula* and pointed to a closed door. "That's his room," said the doorman, as he held up a key ring. "It's probably unlocked, but if not...." He dangled the keys.

Vulso stepped forward and pushed on the door handle. The door swung open and a waft of repulsive smelling air greeted him. Vulso entered quickly, with Crantor and Straton on his heels.

There was the Whale on a chair behind a table. There was no doubt about who it was. He was enormous, fat beyond anyone Vulso had ever seen.

But the Whale didn't react to Vulso's entrance. He couldn't because his head was bent forward, his chin on his chest. There was blood everywhere around his neck. Vulso stepped up to the body and pulled up the Whale's head by his hair. There was a huge slash on his throat from ear to ear. Vulso let go and went back out to the entrance.

"Was he there?" asked Severus. "Did you arrest him?"

"He is there, Judge. But we won't be able to question him. He's dead. Someone slit his throat from ear to ear."

"*Merda,*" exclaimed Severus. He then headed back to the Whale's room and stood in front of the table, looking at the corpse.

"Someone was afraid we'd get to him and that he'd talk. That must have been what happened. Who is that someone? My best guess is *Ipse*. Or an assassin sent by *Ipse*."

"How would *Ipse* know we were so close to finding the Whale?" asked Straton.

"It must have been the fourth assassin who tried to kill me this morning. The one that got away. Probably *Ipse* learned what had happened from him and that two of the assassins were captured and could be made to talk. My guess is that *Ipse* realized we could now find the Whale and since the Whale

knew who *Ipse* was…"   There was no need to elucidate further.

He turned to Vulso and Straton.   "Get the doorman and have him and everyone else in this *insula*
detained and questioned.   Maybe someone knows
something about the Whale's killer, when he was
killed, *et cetera.*   We know the Whale was brought
here in a litter.   Whose litter was it?   Who brought
the Whale here?   Who brought him food?   Who visited him?   Find out whatever you can.   In particular,
I want to know why the Whale was hiding out in this
building.   The *Insula Prisca.*   Is it owned by Octavia
Prisca?   If so, if the Whale went into hiding from
the *Insula Octavia* to the *Insula Prisca*, maybe this is
where Scylax and Baaldo, the *Andromeda* officers, are
hiding as well.   Let's find out."

Severus paced the room, his hands clasped behind
his back, as if oblivious to the bloody corpse dangling
over the table and the smell contaminating the air.

"I'm beginning to figure out this crime," he
said half to himself and half to Vulso and Straton.
"Things are starting to become clearer.   Now I want
to go back to my chambers.   I have to think."

XXI

SCYLAX AND BAALDO ARE FOUND

Vulso and Straton didn't have to send for the *Andromeda*'s owner, Opimius, or its charterer, Antipater, to identify Scylax and Baaldo, the missing officers of the *Andromeda*. Ninnius, the doorman at the *insula* who had told them in which room to find the Whale, volunteered more information.

"If you wanted the Whale, I'm sure you must want his accomplices, Scylax and Baaldo."

Vulso and Straton looked at each other, their eyes lighting up.

"You know where they are?" Vulso said to Ninnius.

"Oh yes," he said with a big grin. "Those mutton heads are on the second floor. In adjoining rooms. They must be in their rooms now because they were there earlier this afternoon and I didn't see either of them leave."

Vulso motioned to the soldiers with him. "The first *contubernium* come with me. The second watch the entrance."

Eight soldiers ascended the stairs behind Vulso, Crantor and Straton, who were following Ninnius. On the second floor, Ninnius pointed to two rooms. Scylax is in the nearest room. Baaldo is in the next one."

Vulso motioned four soldiers to stand next to him in front of Scylax' door, while Straton and the other four soldiers stood at Baaldo's door. Crantor stayed in the hall as back-up.

Vulso nodded to Straton and they each simultaneously pushed open the doors, and burst into the rooms, with the four soldiers behind each of them.

Scylax was lying on his bed along with a young girl. They both bolted up when the intruders entered his room. Vulso pushed Scylax back down on the bed.

"You're under arrest Scylax," said Vulso. "Get up."

Handcuffs were put on him and he was pushed out into the hall.

"Hold him here," said Vulso. "I want to search the room."

Virtually the same thing happened in Baaldo's room. He was lying on his bed along with a young boy. Both stood up when Straton and the troopers burst in. Straton put Baaldo under arrest, handcuffed him and pushed him into the hall and began searching his room.

After completing the searches, Vulso looked at both prisoners. "Scylax. Baaldo. We've been looking for you. Now we're taking you to the chambers of Special Judge Marcus Flavius Severus. Any resistance will be met with painful force. So come along quietly."

Both saw the hard look on Vulso's face and heard the hard tone of his voice. They realized they had been caught and there was nothing they could do about it.

As the prisoners were being led out of the *insula*, Vulso took the doorman aside. "Ninnius, you've been very helpful. I'm sure Judge Severus will show you his appreciation in some meaningful way. But maybe there's some other things you can tell me?"

"What? I'd be very happy to help."

"Do you know who killed the Whale?"

"I don't know, but my best guess is either Scylax or Baaldo. I know they had their heads together when the Whale arrived, heatedly discussing things. I don't know what. Or it could have been that man who visited him yesterday and also this morning, a ruffian, a *grassator*, I thought."

"Can you describe that man?"

"No. Not really. He wore a *paenula* with its hood covering his head and turned his face away so I couldn't see it. That looked suspicious to me."

"Thank you, Ninnius. Now one other thing. Do you know who owns this *insula*? Do you know the Prisca whose name is on the sign outside?"

"The owner is a woman named Octavia Prisca."

When Vulso and Straton returned to the Forum of Augustus and told Judge Severus what they had found out, there were smiles all around.

"Good work, Vulso and Straton. So far, we have recovered the stolen silk. The Whale, who seems to have been instrumental in planning and organizing the crime, is dead. And now we have the missing officers of the *Andromeda*. And most importantly we are closing in on *Ipse*, the one behind the wreck and robbery of the ship."

Severus went into the anteroom and told his court clerk to set up the Tribunal indoors.

"I'm going to hold court now."

A short time later, the 4-foot high platform was set up and the magistrate's curule chair without arms or back was placed on it. Severus donned his judicial toga, with its purple-red hem, mounted the Tribunal, and sat in the curule chair. Two lictors took their place against the wall, holding their bundle of rods. The statue of Jupiter Fidius, the god of Good Faith, was placed in the room. Proculus took a place on the Tribunal next to Severus and readied a pen and scroll to record the proceedings in shorthand. He motioned Vulso and Straton to take other seats on the Tribunal to either side of the judge.

"Now I'll question Scylax and Baaldo. But I'll take Scylax first. He's the senior officer, the *Magister Navis*, the Shipmaster. Bring him in."

XXII

SCYLAX AND BAALDO ARE QUESTIONED IN THE TRIBUNAL AND INVESTORS IN THE ANDROMEDA VOYAGE ARE DISCOVERED

Shipmaster Scylax was brought in first by the lictors and led in front of the Tribunal. He was a man who looked to be in his 40's with a tough weathered face and a tanned complexion. He had a noticeable limp as he walked toward the Tribunal.

"State your name and status in society."

"My name is Lucius Aemilianus Scylax. I was born free and am a Roman citizen." His voice was strong and he looked at the judge directly, without compromise.

"Where are you from? How did you become a Shipmaster?"

"I was born in Tyre into a family of sailors. As a boy I was raised on ships at sea. Sailing merchant ships is my life's work. My father was a ship's captain.

My mother is the daughter of a ship's captain. There is nothing I do not know about merchant ships."

"Do you know how to handle a tiller? Can you steer a ship?"

"Certainly. I am truly a master of a ship, as my title, as *Magister Navis* itself says."

"How did you come to be Shipmaster on the *Andromeda*?"

"The charterer Antipater picked me. I had been Shipmaster for other ships in the past, both Antipater's ships and ships owned by others. For instance, I worked aboard ships owned by Opimius, who owned the *Andromeda*, and also for Zeno, a competitor of Antipater's.

"The *Andromeda* chartered by Antipater was a medium sized merchant vessel chartered in Rome to make a run with one cargo to Alexandria and back to Rome with another. As Shipmaster I saw to it that the vessel was in good condition, the crew was capable, and any other things that needed looking after. It was only at sea, when the *Gubernator*, the Captain, took over that I was not in command, though I remained on the ship throughout the voyage."

"Where were you on the night the *Andromeda* was run aground?"

"I was in my cabin asleep. Demetrios, the Captain, was in charge. I had nothing to do, so I went to sleep."

"When did you become aware that the *Andromeda* had veered onto the shore?"

"When the ship hit the beach, I was jolted awake."

"What did you do?"

"I went out of my cabin and then someone hit me on the head and I lost consciousness."

"Are you aware that is exactly the story told by Captain Demetrios?"

"Yes. I am aware of that. But in my case, it is true. In his, it is not. He must have seen what happened to me and fabricated his story based on what happened to me. He was the person who steered the ship onto the beach."

"How do you know that? According to your story, you didn't see anything. How do you know that Demetrios was at the tiller?"

"He confessed and was convicted. That's how I know."

"When did you regain consciousness?"

"Sometime after the robbery was over. I then wandered dazed until some member of the crew helped me. He and I started walking away from the ship and eventually reached Rome and made it to the *insula* in the Subura where I lived."

"Why didn't you wait at the ship for the authorities to arrive? Why did you leave?"

"I wasn't thinking. I followed the lead of the crew member who helped me out."

"Why didn't you report to Antipater when you reached Rome?"

"I did report to him."

"Why did you move from the *Insula Octavia* in the Subura, to the *Insula Prisca* on the Esquiline?"

"Antipater told me to. He said he was afraid for me, afraid that if I stayed at the *Insula Octavia,* I would be arrested by the authorities and accused of taking part in the beaching of the ship and the robbery. He arranged for me to stay at the *Insula Prisca*."

"Tell me about the Whale. He lived in your apartment building. What did he do there?"

"I don't know. I never talked to him."

"How can I verify any of this? Who was the crewman, for instance, who you say helped you out, led you away from the ship and brought you to Rome? Do you know his name?"

"Actually I do. I heard that he came to the *Insula Octavia* a few days ago looking for me. But he left before I had a chance to see him."

"What was his name?"

"Straton, I think. Yes, Straton. If you find him, he will confirm everything."

"You may step into the anteroom for now. I will recall you later."

Scylax went out followed by one of the lictors.

Severus turned to Straton who was seated on the Tribunal. "Well, Straton, do you confirm everything?"

Everyone laughed.

"What a bald-faced liar," replied Straton. "Can you believe what you just heard? The phony story he made up? I've never heard such outrageous lies."

Severus addressed the other lictor. "Bring in Baaldo."

Baaldo was not as impressive looking at Scylax. He was shorter, thinner and somewhat shifty, with small black eyes. He had trouble standing immobile before the Tribunal. His nerves made him shaky.

"Name and status in society?" asked Severus.

"My name is Baaldo of Sidon, in Phoenicia. I was born free into a family of sailors."

"How did you become Proreus, First Mate, on the *Andromeda*?"

"I was hired by Antipater, the charterer of the ship. I had worked on some of his past voyages and risen to First Mate because of my skills. Sidon is famous for producing seamen and I have lived my life in that tradition. I also had worked for other shipping companies in Rome and Ostia. Occasionally I worked for Opimius, the actual owner of the *Andromeda*. And also for Zeno, one of Antipater's major rivals."

"When the *Andromeda* went aground, where were you?"

"I was asleep in my cabin. It was the middle of the night."

"Do you know who steered the ship into the shore?"

"Yes. It was the Captain Demetrios. I know because he confessed to doing it and was even convicted of it."

"When did you become aware that something was wrong? That the ship was beached?"

"I was thrown out of bed by the ship hitting the beach and breaking apart. I got off the floor headed out. But as I left the cabin, I was hit on the head and knocked unconscious. That's the last I knew until I regained consciousness, when the whole thing was over."

Baaldo then went on to virtually repeat the story that Scylax had foisted on the Tribunal. He had been helped by a crewman, walked to Rome, reported to

Antipater, who arranged he stay at the *Insula Prisca* instead of the *Insula Octavia*. He never spoke to the Whale. The only thing different was that he didn't name Straton as the fellow crewman who could confirm his story.

When Severus finished with him, Scylax was brought back in. Severus looked at them, one after another.

"You are both liars. You will be held in prison here until I decide what to do with you. Maybe torture, certainly a trial, probably a sentence of death in the arena. You can contemplate what's lying store for you.

"And Scylax, you may be interested in knowing that the Straton you named as being the crewman who helped you out is actually a member of the Urban Cohort and is seated right here on the Tribunal. Now get out of here, and think about your painful and dire future, what little of it remains to you."

When they left, Straton made the first comment. "They're liars, no doubt, but one thing they said may be the truth."

"What's that?" asked Vulso.

"When they said that on their return to Rome, they reported in to Antipater, who arranged for them to change their lodgings from the *Insula Octavia* to the *Insula Priscina*."

"If that's true," said Proculus, "then Antipater also lied to us, because he alleged they never reported back to him. He said that's why he concluded that they were dead, not missing."

"Then not just Scylax and Baaldo are liars," concluded Vulso, "Antipater is also."

"And not just them," opined Severus, "because Octavia is probably lying to us too. She must be involved in some important way if the robbers, not to mention the Whale, were staying not just in one of her *insula*e, but at two of them. Could they arrange that without her connivance? And Felix, the recruiter of workers to loot the ship, he had access to the stolen silks. Is Octavia involved in all of this?"

"And if she's involved," added Straton, "what about her cousin and lover Titus Paculus. Maybe he is also involved. Maybe he and Octavia conspired together."

"So is one of them *Ipse*?" asked Vulso. "Is one of them the arch-criminal who planned these crimes? Is one of them the person who arranged for the beaching of the *Andromeda* and the robbery of silks? Is one of them the person who sent assassins to kill you, Judge?"

"Or is it someone else," added Severus. "Someone we haven't considered so far. Someone who appears entirely innocent."

"Speaking of someone who appears innocent and uninvolved," said Proculus, "I've found something interesting among the documents the charterer Antipater brought us."

"What did you find?"

"I found a list of investors in the silk cargo. They included the usual *argentarii*, bankers, *negotiatores*, professional business investors, of course, but there were a few private investors that will interest you."

Here Proculus paused and took a scroll from a *capsa* and unfurled it. "The private investors include Opimius, the owner of the *Andromeda*. He invested a million sesterces. Also, Octavia Prisca invested half a million sesterces and Titus Papirius Paculus invested a million. And Zeno, Antipater's rival over the woman Cassandra. He invested a million sesterces as well."

"Opimius told me about his investment. So did Paculus. But Octavia? She didn't mention it when I talked to her. I wonder why?"

"But there's another investor that you will find even more interesting."

Severus gave him a questioning look. "Who can that be?"

"Septimus Sosius Sulpicius."

"Septimus Sulpicius?" said Severus, still looking inquiringly at his court clerk. "You don't mean Judge Septimus Sulpicius, do you? The judge who presided at the trial of Demetrios?"

"Yes. That's precisely who I mean."

"How much did he invest?"

"Half a million sesterces."

Severus began to think out loud. "So if Demetrios, the Captain appointed by the shipowner Opimius, was guilty of beaching the ship and conspiring with the robbers, then Opimius, having appointed him as his agent, might be liable to investors for their losses. These would include Judge Sulpicius. He could recoup his investment from Opimius. But if Demetrios were innocent, then Judge Sulpicius would simply be out half a million sesterces. So clearly, Judge Sulpicius had a personal interest in seeing Demetrios convicted.

He therefore had a personal interest in ensuring that Demetrios confessed. Yet he told us he had no interest in whether Demetrios was guilty or innocent. He claimed to be neutral. His only interest was justice, he said. So he lied to us too."

Judge Severus shook his head in a negative nod, with a look of disbelief on his face, and threw up his hands in an expressive gesture.

"Is there anyone who is telling us the truth?"

SCROLL V

XXIII

A MASS ARREST OF
ROBBERS IS MADE

It was now the Ides of August, two months after the robbery of the *Andromeda*. And that was the day designated for paying off the money owed to the stevedores and robbers themselves. Or so it was alleged by Hector, the beggar recruited off the streets of Rome by Felix, the compatriot of the Whale. It may have been just 'smoke' to pacify the lowly workers or to cheat them, but it was worth following up.

Accordingly, at the 1st hour of the morning, Felix was brought from his prison cell and seated in the *taberna* of the ex-gladiator Taurus. In the *taberna*, at various tables, were members of the Urban Cohort dressed in ordinary gray or brown tunics, having breakfast drinks of *posca*, hot water with honey and vinegar, and munching on bread and olives and cheese. It was crowded and noisy inside, while it was becoming crowded and noisy outside as people began streaming from their apartments and heading to their work, not just in the Subura itself, but especially in the Imperial forums, abutting the Subura.

Also outside the *taberna*, along with the general public was a large number of the Urban Cohort dressed in civilian tunics and togas. They were there to follow and arrest anyone who had entered the *taberna* and who had received money from Felix. A signal from inside the *taberna* would tell them which exiting person to arrest.

Judge Severus had come to the *taberna* even earlier that morning to talk to Taurus. The ex-gladiator over the years had gotten out-of-shape and pudgy. His once hard, rippling muscles were now noticeably softened. Taurus disliked it when the authorities, especially a Roman judge, showed up and reminded him that he had to cooperate with them or else. But he had been a police informant for more than ten years now and while he hated being one, for ten years he had cooperated.

Severus filled him in on the program. Felix was to be put in a private room upstairs. Anyone who arrived and said the word 'Ajax' must be taken upstairs to see Felix. Taurus was compliant, even though grudgingly. Severus knew that was all an act. Taurus was a reliable informant. He knew where his interests were and where they weren't. The gladiator was still taking counsel of the arena, as the saying went.

Severus, Vulso, and Straton were all seated inside the *taberna* watching what was going on. Felix was taken upstairs to a private room. He had with him a musette bag filled with pouches containing silver *denarii*. For those 'stevedores' like Hector who were owed 80 sesterces, there would be a pouch of 20 denarii. For actual robbers who had raided the beached ship with swords, cutting down anyone who got in the way, there was more than 20 denarii promised. Felix had plenty of pouches in his bag.

To make sure that Felix would follow the program without question, Crantor went with him to the upstairs room. Ostensibly he was there as Felix' bodyguard because Felix had so much money with him. But actually, he was there to watch that Felix did not do or say anything to tip off any of the robbers who came to collect what was owed them. Or to steal some of the money for himself.

When the *taberna* opened at the 1st hour, everyone was in place, both downstairs and upstairs inside the *taberna* and outside on the street. However, no one was sure anyone would turn up. Certainly, anyone who knew Felix had been arrested would stay away, but how many knew that? Maybe no one. Maybe all the robbers and murderers, whoever took part in the crime, would show up unsuspectingly, hoping for a large payoff.

And that's exactly what happened. The hope of scoring a lot of money was too much to resist. So one after another the crooks streamed into the *taberna*, gave Taurus or a waiter the code word 'Ajax' and was brought upstairs. Some had to wait at a table downstairs until Felix finished with one visitor and was free to see the next one. Upstairs, if the robber was recognized by Felix, he would be greeted and given a pouch with money. Each left the *taberna* with a huge smile on his face. However, the smile was wiped off rather quickly after he got out of sight of the *taberna* entrance and was pounced on by police agents. Fear was the main emotion replacing glee as each robber was taken into custody. A few gratuitous punches and smacks during arrests added pain and humiliation to fear.

"How many did we get," asked Severus of the Tribune in charge of the Urban Cohort contingent after it was all over.

"I lost count," replied the officer with a smile. "But it was more than 10, possibly 15. A big day's haul."

"Your men can interrogate them all. You know what we want to know. All the details of the crime. But especially we want *Ipse*, the chief criminal. See if you can find out anything about him. And particularly if anyone of the people we've arrested ever met him or possibly is him. Anyone who met with the Whale is also of interest."

"We'll do the best we can, judge. We have our methods." He didn't have to elaborate. "I'll let you know tomorrow how it went."

The judge thanked him and went home to await news.

That night, after dinner, Artemisia brought up two matters that needed Severus' attention.

"Whose problem to you want to discuss first? Flavia or Alexander?"

"I didn't know Alexander had a problem. What's wrong?"

"He has the same problem as Flavia. They're both in love. Flavia with the slave Bellerephon, and Alexander with Octavia's secretary Persephone."

"When did this happen to Alexander? He only met Persephone the other day. He was supposed to teach her Tironian Notes shorthand and find out what was going on in that house. What happened?"

"What happened was that Persephone not only seduced him, but totally captivated him and turned his head. He's in some sort of reverie. He fell in love, as you Romans say, like a cockroach into a basin. He can't take his mind off her. I've never seen him like this. I brought this up because maybe you might want to talk to him."

"About what? I think it would be good for Alexander to be in love for once with something other than facts. Now tell me what's happening with Flavia?"

"She's over her fake cold and going out every day, spending every day with Bellerephon. She's in love too. But now she has a plan. She's mentioned it to me. She knows that Bellerephon can't be freed from being a slave until he's much older, and she knows that under the law she can't marry a slave and also that any child she might have with him will be a slave and illegitimate under the law. She knows all that and doesn't want any of those things."

"So what's her plan then?"

"She wants to enter into an arranged marriage with someone of the Equestrian Order, like us, or even someone who is a member of the Senatorial Order. But it will be only for show. She then will be able to carry on her affair with Bellerephon, even have his child, but the child will be attributed to her husband and be legitimate and a member of the upper classes. That's her plan."

Severus held his head in his hands. "It's a bad plan."

"She says she would even be willing to marry someone much older as cover. It won't be a real marriage, she says. Maybe we can find someone, she says, who is willing to go along with the arrangement. There may be someone who wants to marry into our family and won't care about anything else. He can have concubines, mistresses, whatever he wants. She wants Bellerephon.

"I told her that plan is deeply flawed. She deserves a real marriage, not a fake one. Her child deserves his real father, not a substitute. Her husband deserves a real wife, not a phantom."

"You're completely correct. What did she say?"

"She said she would think about it. So now, I think you should talk to her."

"I will. Tomorrow."

XXIV

SOME OF THE ROBBERS TALK

Twelve robbers had been arrested outside Taurus' *taberna*. The next morning they were all hauled into the Forum of Augustus and collectively put in front of the Tribunal, where Judge Severus sat, along with court clerk Proculus, who was taking down the proceedings in shorthand.

"I will not mince words with you. The truth is that you are all guilty of murder and all will be tortured and sentenced to death in the arena, unless...."

Here Severus stopped and looked as lowered heads were all raised to look at the Judge with a glimmer of hope. They had all heard the word 'unless'.

Then Severus continued. "...unless you cooperate with me and tell me what I want to know. I am not promising any exoneration or escape from the death penalty. That, you all have earned by committing mass murder. But, as you know, there are horrible lingering ways to die, like excruciating torture followed by being thrown to wild beasts. Or there are quick

deaths by strangling or even beheading, the least onerous, most honorable penalty reserved for members of
the Equestrian and Senatorial Orders. The choice is
yours.

"Now you will all go into holding cells and then
I will call you out one by one. Some of you will, I
know, tell me truthfully what I want to know. Others
will lie. Others may not say anything at all. But rest
assured that some of you will talk and tell me everything. They will receive my consideration. Others
will condemn themselves. And remember, I will know
who is telling the truth and who is lying."

The Judge motioned to the lictors. "Take them
out."

The twelve were put in several holding cells to await
being called back to face the Tribunal. It didn't take
lone. After an hour, the lictors randomly pulled one
of the robbers out of a cell and pushed him back to
the courtroom, placing him in front of Judge Severus.

"State your name and rank in society."

The prisoner remained silent and just glared at
the judge. He was a large strong, tough looking man
and stood in front of the Tribunal, feet splayed apart,
arms crossed in front of him, with a grim, hostile, de-
fiant look on his face.

"State your name and rank in society."

The prisoner once again remained silent, as if
challenging the judge to do something about it.

The question was repeated one more time. This
time the prisoner began to curse the court, the Judge
and all Romans, a scowl on his face and an edge to
his voice.

"You are being disrespectful in and to a Roman court. That is stupid," said the Judge to the prisoner, who kept on cursing, even louder. Severus shrugged his shoulders and looked at the lictors. They knew what to do in cases of open disrespect for a Roman court. Two of the lictors each took a heavy rod from their bundle of rods and approached the prisoner, who stared at them defiantly. Then they began to viciously beat him with the rods until he fell down under the flurry of blows. The prisoner suffered the beating with no sound other than a low groan. After a few more blows to the fallen prisoner's head and body, Severus called a halt and told the lictors to take him out and bring in the next one.

The next one was compliant from the start. "*Eminentissime*, my name is Aures, 'Ears'. I am a free person, born free. I will freely answer your questions. I will tell you whatever you want to know." His tenor was subservient. Perhaps he had seen the last prisoner being dragged out of the courtroom by his feet, perhaps not.

Severus looked at him more closely. He had exceptionally large ears.

"All right, Ears, I want to know all about the robbers who took part in the looting of the beached ship *Andromeda*. Were you part of a robber band, for instance?"

"Yes, *eminentissime*, I was part of a band of robbers that lived in the hills near Laurentum. There were about twenty of us. Some of us are runaway slaves, some runaway criminals and others, like me, poor people who had no jobs. I was once a beggar.

Then I turned to petty crime un Rome, then I joined this gang in the hills. This was three years ago."

"Who headed this gang?"

"His name is Atrox."

"Atrox? Terrible, cruel, atrocious? That's not his real name. What is his real name?"

"We don't use our real names in the gang. My gang name is Aures, although that was also my nickname before I joined the gang. No one knows real names. All I know is that Atrox was the head of the gang. He told us what to do and when to do it. We occasionally robbed lone travelers, but mostly we were hired by people with money who wanted things done. That's what happened here. Atrox told us about a week before we attacked the *Andromeda* that we had been hired to loot a beached ship. Then he introduced someone named Felix to fill us in. Felix told us there would be a cargo ship that would run aground on a beach where we would be waiting. We would loot a cargo of bales of material, he didn't say what material it was, and load them onto waiting wagons to be taken away. He wanted the bales, that's what counted. We were given torches to light up the shore where the ship would see them and be guided onto the beach. The torches were also to provide light so that we could see the cargo we were to loot. We were armed with swords to kill anyone who got in our way, though we were told that the crew would be ordered by someone aboard the ship not to interfere. We were each paid some money in advance and told we would be paid a lot more when the material was sold. The payment would take place two months later at Taurus' *taberna* in the Subura. Felix gave us the code word 'Ajax' and told us that he would personally pay us our money. So that's what he told us, and that's what we did."

"Where is Atrox now?"

Aures looked somewhat surprised. "He is here, *eminentissime*. You just had him in your court. I saw him being dragged back to the cell by his feet."

"That was Atrox?"

"Yes."

Severus motioned to a lictor to remove Aures. "And bring back Atrox."

The lictors went out and came back with Atrox and once again put him in front of the Tribunal. This time his face was smeared with blood.

"Atrox," began the Judge, "I want to reach an understanding with you. I don't care about how you will be executed, slowly and cruelly or quickly and painlessly. I do care about the information you can give me, if you tell me the truth. So I will tell you what I want to know. Then you can answer me now or go back to your cell to think about it until I bring you back tomorrow morning. If you don't answer, I don't even want to contemplate what will happen to you. Your name is Atrox. What will happen to you will be worse than *atrox*, far worse. You have nothing to lose by cooperating with me.

"What I want to know is who hired you to rob the ship. Tell me who that is and answer a few related questions truthfully and I will take your cooperation into consideration on sentencing. Otherwise, you will suffer beyond endurance.

"Will you tell me now who hired you?"

Atrox stood there and looked at the Judge. "I'll think it over," he said gruffly.

"Until tomorrow morning, then," replied Severus, who told the lictors to take him out.

"Do you think he will tell us anything?" asked Proculus.

"I don't know. What do you think?"

"I don't know either. In my long experience in the courts, I know that sometimes even the most recalcitrant relent, sometimes they don't."

"Let's hope Atrox relents."

"Yes. Let's hope. But I wouldn't count on it."

The judge then proceeded to call the captured robbers in front of the Tribunal, one after the other. Some talked a lot and some talked a little, but no one added anything much to Aures' account of the robbery. No one knew who had hired the gang. Everyone said the only person who could give the court the information it wanted was Atrox.

So after a long day in court, Severus returned to his Caelian hill *insula* tired and hungry. But dinner was satisfying. And before he and Artemisia retired that night, Severus went into Flavia's room to talk to her about her relationship with Bellerephon and what the future might hold.

Flavia was strumming on her cithara when Severus came in. She put down the instrument. "Tata, I'm glad you came to talk about this. I want to talk to you about it myself."

"*Pulla*", chickadee, began Severus using a common term of endearment, "your mother told me about the talk you had with her, about your plan to marry some inconsequential person as a cover for your real relationship with Bellerephon and…"

"I've given up that plan," she interrupted. "I realize I will have no real marriage; any child I have with Bellerephon cannot be acknowledged or raised by his real father; the person who marries me, if I can find one, will not have a real marriage, and I will be ostracized by most people in society because I couldn't keep the arrangement a secret. Not in gossipy Rome.

"So I talked to Bellerephon about it. He wants us to run away together and live somewhere else under assumed names. I told him I can't do that. I love my parents and my *familia* and my friends and I don't want to leave them. I don't want to live an artificial, made-up, hidden life. I want my own life. He asked me what we should do then. I told him we would have to break up. I told him I love him and I know he loves me, but the world we live in doesn't permit me to marry or have legitimate children with a slave. And he can't be freed until he is past 30 under the law, and in all reality I can't wait more than ten years to marry and have children. Perhaps at that time, we can see where we are in life and possibly renew our relationship. But for now we have to end it, I told him. He objected, he argued with me, he pleaded. We both feel terrible about it. I cried, he cried. But I know I must be strong."

Flavia was on the point of tears several times as she spoke, but she managed to control her emotions, though intermittently wiping her eyes with a handkerchief.

Severus was impressed by his daughter's desire to be sensible, pragmatic and a Stoic. These were Roman virtues that everyone tried to inculcate into their children, both boys and girls. He hugged her and told her how proud he was of her. He knew how she must suffer because of her decision and assured her that she would find someone else, but someone else of her class in this class-minded society, someone she would love and who would love her. She would have a real marriage with legitimate children.

"I couldn't be more proud of you, *Pulla*."

"Thank you, Tata. I will go and tell Mama right now."

"She will be proud of you too."

Later that night in bed, Severus and Artemisia talked over what had happened.

"I'm really proud of Flavia," said Severus, feeling relieved. "I know how difficult it must be for her."

"I'm proud of her decision too," replied Artemisia. "But I'm not exactly counting on it."

"What do you mean?"

"Just what I said."

They both went to sleep, somewhat relieved, but still somewhat worried.

XXV

ATROX BEFORE THE TRIBUNAL

Court was convened precisely at the 3rd hour the next day. Judge Severus and his court clerk sat on the Tribunal and Atrox was placed in front of it.

Severus looked directly at Atrox. "What have you decided?"

Atrox took a moment to reconsider what he had decided to do. Then he bit his lip, contorted his face into a grimace of displeasure and said, "I'll cooperate."

"Who hired you?"

"I was first contacted by someone named Felix, who said he had a job for our gang. This was several months ago. I don't remember the date exactly. Felix was sent to us by someone who had hired our gang in the past and whose recommendation we could trust. Anyway, Felix said his boss would discuss the job with me in detail and took me to an *insula* in the Subura to meet him. Once there, I was taken to see the fattest person I ever saw. Someone named the Whale."

Atrox stopped. "Can I have some water?"

A lictor went out and brought a pitcher of water and a cup and poured one into the other. Atrox drank and then continued.

"The Whale told me of a plan he had. He said there would be a merchant ship with a cargo of silks from *Seres* coming to Ostia. He would let me know more precisely when later on. He said there were officers aboard who were willing and able to beach the ship at night. Once ashore, the ship could be raided and looted. He said he needed a gang on shore that could carry out that part of the plan. That is, taking the silk off the ship and transporting it to the Urbs.

"He asked me where would be a good spot to beach the ship. I told him there was a shore north of Laurentum that would be perfect. I said we could have torches light up the beach if we knew when the ship would be there. He said he would know when the ship got close. His accomplices aboard would get a message out by semaphores to alert us to what night the ship would be passing by Laurentum. We discussed details. He seemed totally knowing about the plan. I assumed he was in charge of everything. But then he told me that in reality he wasn't. He said someone he would only call *Ipse* was giving him orders. He never said who *Ipse* was, but told me I didn't have to know and would never meet him.

"I asked the Whale who aboard the ship would beach it. He said again I didn't have to know, but since I had to meet with an accomplice during the operation to carry out the final part of the plan, he said the *Proreus,* the First Mate, was one of them. He called him Baaldo and described him to me. He was not the only one, the Whale said. I was also to provide two large *carpenta* coaches to take Baaldo and other con-spirators along with the silks to Rome. They would tell the driver where to go in Rome and supervise the unloading of the cargo.

"We then discussed payments and reached an agreement easily enough. The Whale offered me and my gang a quarter of a million sesterces for our par-ticipation. A huge sum and more than we ever made anywhere, anytime. We would get some money up front, but the bulk would be paid later when the silks were sold. I readily agreed.

"We discussed recruiting 'stevedores' who would unload the cargo while our gang took care of anyone who got in the way. The First Mate would order the crew to remain in place, not to interfere. The Whale told me Felix would supply 'stevedores' and would arrange their transportation to where our gang was. Felix would coordinate everything."

Atrox stopped, as if finished. Severus, however, began to ask questions.

"How many conspirators did you take to Rome with the silks? Who were they?"

"Just one other besides Baaldo went into one of the coaches. I don't know his name. He was an older man and walked with a limp."

Severus immediately knew it was the Shipmaster Scylax who was being described, as he remembered Scylax limping when he walked to the Tribunal a few days before.

"How many people did your gang kill during the robbery?"

"I have no idea. Anyone who got in the way was cut down. It was dark and people were running helter-skelter all over the place. Whoever was in the wrong place at the wrong time paid the price."

"Did the Whale say anything else about *Ipse* that you can remember."

"Just what I told you. I got the impression that *Ipse* was the master criminal behind this whole plan. The Whale was his chief underling in charge of all the arrangements. The Whale talked to everyone. *Ipse* talked only to the Whale."

Severus then went through Atrox' testimony again to see if the story he told would be the same the second time around. A basic interrogatory tactic. Atrox' first and second telling had no discrepancies. It seemed he might be telling the truth.

XXVI

MARCUS FLAVIUS
SEVERUS: TO HIMSELF

I gathered everyone together the next evening in my
home. Artemisia, Vulso, Straton, Flaccus, Crantor,
Alexander and Proculus. We agreed we had now
reached an impasse. Were the Whale still alive, we
could squeeze information out of him. Who was *Ipse*?
He could tell us and would tell us under torture. To
prevent that was the reason he was killed, we believed.

Who killed him? Probably either Scylax or Baaldo
was the perpetrator or both together. They were both
hiding out in the *Insula Prisca* with the Whale and
they were both complicit in the robbery of the ship,
according to Atrox. So they might well have been
afraid that we would find and arrest the Whale and
force him to talk about them. *Cui bono*? As judges ask
in the courts. To who's good? Who benefits? In other
words, who has a motive. And Scylax and Baaldo had
good motives to kill the Whale. To protect themselves.

But they weren't the only ones. *Ipse*, himself, had the best motive because he met personally with the Whale. The Whale coordinated and directed whatever *Ipse* told him to do. The Whale had a direct link to *Ipse*. Only the Whale, as far as we knew, could identify *Ipse*. Therefore, the Whale must be silenced before he could be arrested.

The doorman at the *Insula Prisca* said the Whale was visited twice by someone he called a ruffian, a *grassator*, once on the day before and then on the morning before he was found dead. Who was he? Was he possibly the other assassin *Ipse* sent to kill me? Was he Furius, the person named by Kastor, the assassin we captured?

And why was the Whale killed when he was killed? I asked rhetorically. And then gave an answer. I reconstructed what happened. It was the attack on me in the park that must have sparked it. The assassin who ran away, Furius, must have reported not only the failure of the attack, but also that two others of their band had been captured, the fourth having been killed. Likely Furius first reported to the Whale. That was the first visit of the ruffian with the Whale the day before. Then probably Furius reported to *Ipse* what had happened. Maybe the Whale thought he was safe hiding in a different *insula*, but maybe *Ipse* thought differently and ordered him killed. That was the second visit of the ruffian with the Whale, on the morning of the Whale's murder. Furius may be the killer of the Whale, maybe alone or maybe with the aid of Scylax and Baaldo.

What about Octavia? Artemisia asked. She owns both the *Insula Octavia* where the Whale, Scylax and Baaldo all lived and planned the robbery of their ship. And then she also owns the *Insula Prisca*, where all three went to hide out. Didn't she know about all this? Does she have a role in it? If so, what is it? Is she as innocent of what went on in her *insulae* as she pretends? Or could she even be *Ipse*?

To be technical, Alexander pointed out, it should be Herself, *Ipsa*, instead of Himself, *Ipse*. But it hardly needed to be said that *Ipsa* would be a give-away. Criminals were interested in concealment, not grammar.

And if Octavia were involved, what about Senator Paculus? asked Flaccus. He was the patron of Antipater, the charterer of the *Andromeda* and also the lover of Octavia. Could the lovers, Paculus and Octavia, be conspiring with each other? Were they both together operating under the rubric of one person, *Ipse*? Or was Paculus himself *Ipse*?

We didn't know the answers to these questions. And for all we knew, *Ipse* might be someone unknown to us.

Which brings to mind, said Alexander, someone we've not considered. I mean the rival of Antipater, Zeno. They had a falling out over a woman, and Antipater thinks that Zeno was involved in the crime. What do we know about him? I answered that we had not one single shred of evidence against this Zeno.

And what about Antipater himself, suggested Flaccus. Could he be involved in some way?

It's not very likely, replied Proculus. Why would anyone steal from himself what he already owns? There was no answer to that question.

What would we have to do then to get the answers then? What must be the next steps in our investigation?

The floor was open to suggestions.

Straton thought we should question Scylax and Baaldo again about the murder of the Whale. Maybe they knew the ruffian described by the doorman, the fourth assassin, who visited the Whale twice. Maybe they all cooperated together in the murder of the Whale?

I turned to my court clerk. Put that on the calendar. A Tribunal session with Scylax and Baaldo about the killing of the Whale.

Next, I suggested, we have to explore further the involvement of Octavia and Senator Paculus. Put them on the calendar as well, though I won't haul them before the Tribunal. I'll talk to them separately, one after the other on the same day. I don't want one telling the other of my interview in advance of theirs. I'll take them on first. Scylax and Baaldo are prisoners. I can question them any time.

So that's how we decided to proceed.

XXVII

SEVERUS QUESTIONS
PACULUS AND OCTAVIA

Senator Paculus arrived at Severus' chambers in the Forum of Augustus in an 8-bearer litter with modern sliding translucent glass windows. Alongside walked an entourage of 12 people, freedmen and slaves. The display was to show his status, his prestige and his wealth.

Severus was not impressed. To the contrary, he thought it overdone and was put off by it. Was Paculus trying to intimidate me? Severus thought to himself. He made a little laugh to himself. If so, he picked the wrong person. Nevertheless, they politely exchanged greeting kisses.

Still Paculus, dressed in a freshly laundered very white toga over a tunic displaying the broad reddish-purple stripe of the Senatorial Order, sauntered into the chambers as if he owned the place. "I brought a fine old Massic to drink during whatever it is you have in mind." He motioned to one of his slaves who put a bottle of wine and two glasses on the table between him and the judge. "I invite you to join me."

"*Clarissime*, last time we talked," began Severus, "you anticipated all my questions and answered without me even having to voice them."

"*Eminentissime,* I will do it again. You are desperately trying to find out who *Ipse* is. Am I right? Of course, I am. Also, I am one of the suspects. You think I might be *Ipse*. But you are wrong. I am not *Ipse*. But I know who he is."

Severus knew immediately, of course, how Paculus knew he was suspected of being *Ipse*. It was precisely what Severus had told Alexander to tell Persephone, and what he had told her in exchanging confidences. Persephone had obviously reported what Alexander said to Octavia and Octavia had obviously passed it on to Paculus. Octavia and Paculus were not just lovers, they were exchanging information relating to the *Andromeda* affair.

"Senator, you just said you know who *Ipse* is. Who is he?"

"He's my freedman and former slave Antipater."

"Antipater? You mean the charterer of *Andromeda* and owner of the silks that were stolen?"

"Yes. Him."

"Why should he steal what he already owns?"

"I thought you might ask that question, Judge, and I have an answer."

"Let's hear it,"

"He didn't own the entire shipment of silks. He had investors to pay off. He would make a profit, for sure, but not as large a profit as if he owned all the silks. By stealing them, he owns it all and can sell them for their full value without having to pay off any investors. Then by having the Captain convicted of wrecking the ship, he can have the owner of the ship, Opimius, reimburse him for the value of the stolen silks. So he would profit doubly from stealing what he already owns."

"Not a very convincing plan. First of all, he is not certain of getting reimbursed by the ship's owner. Opimius will contest it in court and those kinds of cases can take years before the courts reach a decision. Secondly, there is no guarantee that everything would go according to plan, that he would actually be able to sell all the stolen silk. In fact, I now have his silk, not him. Third, it seems totally unreasonable to go to all the trouble of hiring a gang of robbers, murdering people, unloading the cargo, storing it and having to sell it all for not very much profit over what he is going to make by not robbing his own ship. I am unconvinced."

Paculus looked miffed at Severus' rejection of his idea. He didn't like being contradicted by anyone. He looked away and took a gulp of wine.

"If that's the way you think, Judge, then I have another thought about who *Ipse* is."

Severus made a hand motion indicating he should go on.

"Zeno did it. My other freedman. The person who once was a friend of Antipater until they fell out over the woman Cassandra."

"Oh yes. You told me you had them toss dice to see who would have Cassandra and Antipater won."

"That's right. And because of it, Zeno hates Antipater and so arranged to rob his valuable cargo of silk."

"What evidence do you have that Zeno did it?"

"None, actually, but it's your job to find the evidence."

"Any other people you believe might be *Ipse*?

"I can tell you one who isn't. Me. You must absolve me of being *Ipse* because, as I told you before, I invested money in the *Andromeda*'s voyage. So, your opinion should be that I also would not steal what I already own"

Severus refreshed himself with a sip of wine. "You have a point there. But it's not exactly analogous. You didn't own the silk. You only invested in the enterprise. You had much less to lose than Antipater. And by the way, Senator, how much did you invest?"

"A quarter of a million sesterces."

That answer stopped Severus in his tracks. He already knew from the documents about the investors in the *Andromeda*, that Paculus had invested a million sesterces. Not a quarter of a million. Why is he lying about the sum? Severus made a neutral comment.

"That's a lot of money."

Paculus shrugged his shoulders. "I suppose it is to some people." His tone was arrogant.

"You don't like Antipater much, do you? Or Zeno?"

"I hate both of them, if you want to know the truth. Antipater is always trying to lord it over me because he is so wealthy. This despite the fact that he is a freedman, a former slave, while I am a member of the Senatorial Order. What arrogance on his part!"

Severus saw the irony. Was it the freedman who was arrogant, as the Senator alleged? Or was it the Senator who was arrogant, as any freedman would think. Keeping his thoughts to himself, the judge stayed on the subject.

"If you hated him so much, how is it that you invested so much money in the silk from *Seres* he was bringing to Rome?"

"Antipater makes money. Lots of money. It seemed like a good investment."

"And what about Zeno? Why do you hate him?"

"On general principles I find him unpleasant, unlikeable. He also thinks he's better than me."

"Now, let's discuss whether you are *Ipse*."

"All right. Let's discuss it. Why do you suspect me?"

"Your cousin Octavia's name keeps coming up in connection with people who were in the conspiracy. The Shipmaster Scylax, for one, the First Mate Baaldo and their boss the Whale. They all lived in one of Octavia's *insulae* and hid out in another. Didn't Octavia know about this?"

"Oh yes, them. I don't know what Octavia knew. In any case, what do they have to do with me, or put it better, what do I have to do with them? I never met any of them."

"But your cousin Octavia is also your mistress. Is that not true?"

"Yes. I know you know that already. When you visited her home, she wore her see-through silk *stola,* didn't she? Then you saw how alluring she is. She's even more alluring without it on. But, may I ask, so what? You probably think she might be *Ipse*, or should I say *Ipsa*, as well. How dreary. You're just chasing phantoms."

"How do you know so much about my investigation?" Severus was fishing because he already knew Paculus must have heard it from Octavia, who got it from Persephone, who was told it by Alexander. But he wanted to see how Paculus would reply.

"I prefer not to tell you. I do not want to compromise my sources, after all."

"Now, Senator, I want to ask you about your whereabouts when some of the events in this case happened. The beaching of *Andromeda*, for instance, or when I was attacked in the park, or…"

Paculus held up an open palm to stop him from going on. "Whatever you ask, Judge, I was at home. I am always at home. Either there or at a gambling house. And I have numerous slaves who will support what I say. And you can't torture them for evidence because, as you well know, slaves can't testify against their masters. So any question you ask me about my whereabouts will be answered in the same way. I was at home or at a gambling house. And I have numerous slaves to back me up."

"Where do you go to gamble?"

"I'm not sure I should say. Isn't it true that there is still a law on the books from the time of the Republic banning gambling except at the Games or during the Saturnalia? You are trying to trap me."

"Yes, that law is still on the books, but it was hardly ever enforced during the Republic and is never enforced now in the Empire. After all, the Emperor Augustus held gambling parties on the Palatine, as did some other emperors as well. So it's a defunct law and no, I'm not trying to trap you. I'm just curious about where you go to gamble."

"I gamble at a few places. Sometimes, at a private home. Sometimes at a *taberna* with a gambling hall. Sometimes at a brothel with a gambling room. It depends on my mood. And by the way, Judge, I brought my dice box with me. I'm hoping you now want to gamble, for real money this time."

"No. I'm not interested in gambling, as I've already told you. It's fruitless to ask me again. But maybe you think you're playing a game with me about the identity of *Ipse*. I find that suspicious."

"That is your problem, Judge."

"No, Senator, it is your problem."

Paculus got up and left. Severus noted that he didn't pay the measly 1 sesterce he owed him from the one time they threw dice. Just like he heard about compulsive gamblers. Untrustworthy. Slimy. All that counts for them is money and their strange up and down emotional life.

A few hours after Paculus left, Octavia arrived. This time she was not dressed in her see-through silk *stola*, but in a modest, everyday linen *stola*. She was accompanied by her private secretary Persephone.

"Please wait in the anteroom, Persephone," asked the Judge. "I want to talk to Octavia alone." Octavia nodded at her secretary who got up and went into the anteroom.

"I'm distressed," began Severus, when they were alone, "that your name and your *insulae* keep coming up in connection with the robbery of *Andromeda*."

"I had nothing to do with that at all. I know nothing about it."

"I am also disturbed by your pose of innocence. You cannot be as unaware as you pretend to be. You are not a child, after all. And then you are the mistress of Titus Paculus, who brags about how much he knows. If he knows so much, and you are intimate with each other, you cannot be without knowledge. I just don't believe it. So, it's now time to tell me what you know."

"About what? What do you want to know?"

"First, tell me what you know about the Whale. How come he lived in your *insula* and took care of affairs for you there?"

"I inherited the Whale along with the *insula*. My husband hired him years ago and gave him a place to live in the *insula* in exchange for taking care of the building. The Whale was smart and competent and because he was so fat, he was always on the premises. What more could one want of an agent?"

"How often did you talk to the Whale?"

"Not very often. I usually had one of my slaves deal with the Whale and take care of what needed fixing. The Whale also collected rents and gave it to my slave."

"Who among the residents at the *insula* do you know?"

"No one, really. I have no reason to talk to anyone other than the Whale, and I never did."

"So you don't know Scylax or Baaldo, for instance."

"I never met them or even heard of them until this business with the *Andromeda* came up. You say they conspired with the Whale. I know nothing about that at all. I only met with the Whale. No one else."

"How is it then that when the Whale fled the *Insula Octavia*, he fled to the *Insula Prisca*, which you also own. And how is it that Scylax and Baaldo, once residents of the *Insula Octavia*, hid out in the *Insula Prisca*?"

"I don't know. The Whale, of course, knew about all my properties. Maybe it was natural for him to send his accomplices to hide out there. Maybe it was the logical place for him to go when he thought he was in danger of being taken into custody at the *Insula Octavia*"

"How much is your cousin and lover, Titus Paculus, involved in your affairs?"

"I don't know how to answer that. We are intimate. However, he has nothing to do with my business affairs and I have nothing to do with his."

"Don't you two ever discuss your business problems with the other? Seek advice about them?"

"No, when we are together, we have more enticing things to do than talk about business."

"But there must have been some business discussed between you and your cousin, mustn't there? You both invested in the *Andromeda* cargo of silks. How did that come about?"

She didn't miss a beat. "In two ways, actually. The Whale recommended the investment to me. And

I recommended it to Titus. But he had already heard about the shipment from Antipater. So we both invested in the enterprise. And we've both lost our investments. It is very distressing for me. I'm not all that wealthy. Of course, it's much worse for Titus."

"How is that? Isn't he very rich?"

"He pretends to be. But he's a compulsive gambler. And like all compulsive gamblers he loses and loses and loses. He's lucky that Antipater gives him money to pay off his gambling debts. Otherwise, he would have nothing. He certainly wouldn't have the million sesterces needed to qualify as a member of the Senatorial Order. Not even the 400,000 sesterces needed to qualify as a member of the Equestrian Order. And now, with the loss of his investment, he may also lose his status in society."

"He didn't seem that desperate to me, when he was here earlier today."

"It's an act. He is now truly desperate."

"Is there anything else you can tell me?"

"Just this. You say you are distressed by what you call my pose of innocence. I am distressed by having been betrayed by the Whale, who evidently carried out criminal enterprises from my *insula*. I am also distressed that residents of my *insula* were his accomplices, and that they also used another of my *insulae* to hide out from the law. I am also distressed at being suspected by you for heading these crimes. I know nothing about them. It is not a pose of innocence. It is a fact that you should accept. Stop suspecting me and find the person who is the real culprit, the real perpetrator of these crimes."

Severus smiled in appreciation of her little speech. "You would have made a good advocate in the courts, Octavia. Did you ever think about becoming a lawyer?"

The implication was clear to Octavia. The judge regarded her peroration as nothing more than practiced legal argumentation. As much false as true, whatever fit the occasion.

"Actually, I did once. But I got married instead. While it's not impossible, it's difficult for a woman to become a lawyer. It's easier to become a wife. But perhaps the one is as stressful as the other." With that, the session ended.

XXVIII

SCYLAX AND BAALDO ARE AGAIN SUMMONED TO THE TRIBUNAL

Before the court session, Severus discussed with his assessor Flaccus and court clerk how they would deal with Scylax and Baaldo.

"When we last had them in court," recalled Severus, "they both alleged that they were asleep when the *Andromeda* was beached and that they were hit on the head when they left their cabins, mimicking the story of the Captain. That was a lie. They were not bystanders. They were accomplices, as we learned from Atrox, the robber chief.

"Then they said that they went back to Rome by foot. That was a lie. They were actually transported back to Rome in coaches along with the stolen silks.

"Then they said they reported to Antipater, who told them to hide out in the *Insula Prisca*. That may also have been a lie, because Felix told us that it was the Whale who told them to hide out there.

"They also lied that a crewman named Straton would corroborate their fables, not knowing, of course, that Straton was a member of the Urban Cohort and was actually seated on the Tribunal that day."

"So we have them in many lies," said Flaccus. "What do we want to find out?"

"One, their real role in the shipwreck and robbery. Two, their collusion with Atrox. Three, their collusion with the Whale. Four, who killed the Whale?"

"What's your plan then?" asked Flaccus.

"I'm going to tell Baaldo that he was accused of being the guilty by Scylax, who claimed to be innocent, and Scylax that he was fingered by Baaldo."

"This I have to see," said Proculus.

Severus ordered the lictors to bring Scylax and Baaldo from the prison to the Tribunal. "I want you to bring them here together and then put them in separate cells, out of the sight of each other. Wait an hour and then bring Baaldo to stand alone in front of the Tribunal. And, by the way, you don't have to be gentle when bringing them here."

The lictors took Severus' suggestion in the manner it was intended. While escorting them from prison, they bound the prisoners so tightly that it hurt. Then they slapped the prisoners around, kicked them, pushed them hard, yelled at them and generally mistreated them on the way to court.

Scylax and Baaldo were then isolated from each other. After an hour was up, the lictors hauled Baaldo in front of the Tribunal. Baaldo stood there, his head hung down, not daring to look at the judge.

Severus addressed him in a harsh, fearsome voice from his elevated seat on the Tribunal.

"Look at me, you viper." Baaldo raised his head. Severus gazed directly into his eyes. "I know about your lies. You think you can put something over on this court? You're wrong. Let me tell you how you lied and how I know it."

Severus then proceeded to tell him.

"It was you who steered the *Andromeda* onto the beach. It was you who hit the Captain on the head when he emerged from his cabin. You were the one who ordered the crew not to interfere with the robbery. This whole crime had been planned by you and the Whale ahead of time. Then you didn't walk to Rome, as you alleged, but were driven there in a coach with the stolen silks. It was not Antipater, but the Whale who told you to hide out at the *Insula Prisca*. It was you who murdered the Whale."

Baaldo looked at the judge with an open mouth, as if he wanted to protest.

But Severus continued. "How do I know all this? Because in the last hour, while you were in a jail cell, your good friend Scylax told me the whole story. He told me how you were the real perpetrator of this crime. You and the Whale."

"That dirty, lying pile of shit. It was him, not me. He was the one who planned the whole thing, along with the Whale. He roped me into it. He was the one who steered the ship onto the beach in the middle of the night. He killed the helmsman and took over the tiller. He did it. Not me.

"As for killing the Whale, I don't know why he accused me. Yes, I was in the room, as was Scylax, but it was Furius who cut the Whale's throat from behind. Not me. I didn't even know he was going to do it. I…"

Severus held up his hand to stop him. Furius, Severus already knew, was the name of the assassin who ran away as the attempt to kill him in the park was failing. Furius, according to his fellow-assassin Kastor, was the one who led the attempt. He was not a henchman of the Whale as the other three were, but was sent by *Ipse*.

"Who is Furius?" asked Severus in order to test Baaldo's account.

"He's from *Ipse*. He often relays *Ipse*'s orders to the Whale. That's who he is. It took me by surprise when Furius killed the Whale. I swear this by Jupiter and all the gods. Also, I swear by Jupiter and all the gods that it was Scylax who plotted this whole crime with the Whale. He is the real criminal. Not me. Not me. He's the Shipmaster. I'm only the lowly First Mate."

"Get him out of here," said Severus to the lictors. Two of them took Baaldo back to his cell. Severus turned to the other two lictors. "Now bring in Scylax."

When Scylax was before the Tribunal, Severus used the same tactic on him. Only, of course, he substituted Scylax for the perpetrator of the ship beaching and the murderer of the Whale, and said that it was Baaldo who had confessed and named him.

"That dirty rotten liar. It was he who killed the helmsman and steered the ship onto the beach. And I don't know why he accused me of killing the Whale.

He was in the room, as I was, when Furius murdered the Whale. Furius had us come with him to distract the Whale by talking to him, while Furius could sneak up behind and cut his throat. But I didn't know beforehand that Furius intended to kill the Whale."

"Who ordered Furius to kill the Whale? Was it *Ipse*?"

"I don't know who else it could be. But I never met *Ipse*. Only the Whale did."

When Baaldo was removed from the court. Severus turned to Proculus and Flaccus, seated on the Tribunal with him. Flaccus spoke first.

"Who killed the Whale? Scylax and Baaldo say it was Furius. Do you believe them, Judge? Or are they just covering up for themselves by pinning it on someone else."

"I believe them. It all seems to fit together. Furius led the attempt to assassinate me and ran away when it failed. He must have reported to *Ipse* what happened, and *Ipse* realized that one or more of the assassins we captured would talk and give up the Whale. We would then squeeze out of the Whale who *Ipse* was. So the Whale had to be silenced. That's the way it seems to shape up."

"What about Scylax and Baaldo? They say they were in the room distracting the victim when Furius cut his throat."

Proculus commented. "From my long experience in the courts, in cases like this, it makes no difference. They are both accomplices in the murder. Distracting the victim is part of the crime. Both are guilty. Both deserve to die."

"I couldn't agree with you more," said the Judge.

"But each says he is innocent, that he didn't know beforehand that Furius was going to kill the Whale," objected Flaccus. "You can't convict an innocent person."

"In this case," rejoined Severus, "I don't believe either of them is innocent. They say they didn't know Furius was going to kill the Whale. But why should I believe that to be true? I think the truth is that they knew very well what was going to happen to the Whale. They were all accomplices and all are guilty of murder. And I can and will convict them both. After a trial, of course."

"Oh yes, a trial is necessary," put in Proculus. "If a defendant wants it, Roman justice requires a trial."

"What a waste of time," said Flaccus, almost scornfully.

"It may be a waste of time from the point of view of efficiency," observed Severus, "but my court clerk is right. It is necessary to observe the forms of the judicial system. That is part of justice. It is not just the verdict that counts, but the way the verdict was reached counts too."

"But you've made up your mind already, even before a trial." countered Flaccus. "How does your view of justice cope with that?"

"My mind is still open. As of now I will convict them both. But if there is a trial, I will listen to and consider any defense. Perhaps my mind will be changed."

"But that's not very likely, is it?"

"No. It's not very likely at all. In any event, even if there is some doubt about the extent of their involvement in the murder the Whale, we have them both for murder at the beached ship. That's enough for a sentence of death."

"But we're not any closer to finding out who *Ipse* is," said Flaccus. "What are we going to do about that? The Whale is dead, so we know of no one who can identify the Whale."

"That's not exactly true," replied the Judge, "we now know of someone else who can tell us who *Ipse* is."

Flaccus and Proculus looked at him with inquiring eyes.

"Furius. Furius can tell us."

"But where can we find Furius?" asked Flaccus.

"We can start by quizzing the other assassin we captured. Kastor says he knows that Furius got his orders from the Whale. But the other one, the one that Argos leaped on and brought down, maybe he knows something."

"It's an idea, at any rate," commented Flaccus. Then he laughed as an idea came to him. "Make sure you bring your dog to court for the interrogation,"

"I'll even have Argos sit on the Tribunal," replied Severus, pleased at the idea.

SCROLL VI

XXIX

THE HUNT FOR FURIUS

The next day, at the 3rd hour of the morning, the assassin who Argos had brought down was brought before the Tribunal. Severus sat on the magistrate's curule chair, with Flaccus on one side and Proculus on the other. Between Severus and Proculus was Argos, obeying his 'sit' command, with a bowl of water in front of him. He recognized the man coming to stand in front of him and made a low menacing growl. The assassin recognized Argos and cowered. His hands and face were not yet recovered from bites. They still hurt. And Argos was the main monster in his nightmares.

"Name and status?" asked Severus.

"My name is Borvo. I was born free and am a Roman citizen."

"Borvo? What kind of name is that?"

"Borvo is a god of healing among the Gauls. My ancestors were prisoners of war, long since freed. I am a descendant."

A Shipwreck Conspiracy

"Why did you try to assassinate me?"

"I was hired to do it."

"By whom? The Whale?"

"No, not the Whale. I only met him once, before going out to do the job. My boss was Furius, the one who ran away. He hired me."

"Who hired him?"

"I don't know. I know he worked for someone high up. Furius got his orders from him and was told to contact the Whale, who had two others who would come along with us. That's all I know."

"Have you done jobs like this before?"

Borvo was silent.

"Well, have you?"

"Not killings. Only small robberies and burglaries. I've never killed anyone."

Severus didn't believe him. He was obviously a cutthroat who worked for anyone who would pay him. But the Judge had more important things to find out than Borvo's criminal past.

"Where can I find Furius?"

"I don't know."

"You'd better rethink that answer," said Severus, whose voice and glare were sharpening. "I want Furius. If you help me find him, it will be to your benefit. If not, you will suffer the consequences. I mean horrible torture, a long and painful death. You've seen it all. Everything like that, torture and executions, are all done in the open in Rome. You will be tortured and killed for the enjoyment of scum like you."

Borvo thought it over.

"I don't know where he lives, although I know it's somewhere in the Subura. I sometimes run into him in a *taberna* where he likes to hang out."

"What *taberna*? Where is it?"

"It's the *taberna* of an ex-gladiator named Taurus. It's near…"

"I know where it is," interrupted the Judge. "Describe Furius to me. What does he look like?"

"I don't know how to describe him. Not too tall, not too short, not too thin or fat. Just regular. He looks tough, though."

"I will have an artist brought to your cell. This artist will draw a picture of Furius according to your description. You will tell him the shape of Furius' face, the look of his eyes, nose, ears, mouth. You will adjust the details of the drawing as they're being done. You know the procedure, I'm sure. We will end up with an accurate painting of what he looks like and people will be able to identify him from it. Your fate depends on the accuracy of your description and the extent of your cooperation."

Severus motioned to a lictor to remove Borvo from the court.

By later that afternoon, a painting of a recognizable man was in the hands of the Judge.

"Let's have a drink at Taurus' *taberna*," he said to Vulso and Crantor. "We'll see if Taurus knows this viper."

The three walked together to Taurus' *taberna* and found Taurus as usual greeting customers. And as usual, Taurus was not pleased to see the Judge or

Vulso, but went with them up the stairs to his office on the mezzanine.

"What can I do for you,Judge?"

Vulso unrolled the painting. "Do you know him?"

Taurus didn't need anything but a quick glance. "Yes. He comes in here occasionally. His name is Furius."

"How often does he come here?"

"I'm not sure. I'd say maybe once in 10 days or so. Something like that."

"When was the last time he was in here?"

"A few days ago, I think. I'm not sure. I can ask the waiters."

"Where does he live?"

"I don't know. Somewhere in the Subura."

"I want Furius," said Severus. "I want you to ask your waiters, your musicians, your dancing girls, anyone and everyone in this *taberna*, if necessary. I want to know who knows him, and where he can be found. This is important to me. Your cooperation will be greatly appreciated and rewarded."

"I can start right now." Taurus went to the door of his office and called for one of the staff. "Gaius, I want you to bring every staff member, waiter, cook, musician, dancing girl, slave, one by one, up here. Now."

Gaius came back leading a waiter. "Look at this painting. It's of Furius. He's often in here. Do you know him?"

The waiter scanned the painting. "Yes, I've seen him in here. But I don't know his name or anything about him."

"Bring up another," instructed Taurus.

In the next hour, they ran through 15 slaves, musicians, waiters, staff and dancing girls without learning anything new. Most recognized Furius, a few even knew his name, but no one had anything new to say about him. No one until a Spanish dancing girl named Stena saw the painting.

"It's Furius. That rat."

"Why do you call him a rat?" asked Severus.

"Because he mistreated me. That's why. One night, maybe a few months ago, I went back with him to his apartment. He paid me enough to spend the night. More than enough. So first he poked me, that's what he paid for. But then he beat me up. Then he poked me some more. That's why I call him a rat. There's was no need to beat me up. I think he enjoyed beating me up more than poking me. The rat."

"Where does he live?"

"Not far from here. I always remember where I'm taken so I can find it later, if I need to go back, either for seconds or for revenge. I can take you there, if you want."

"Yes. Now. Let's go."

Stena then led the way out of the *taberna*, turning down one side street and into another. They reached a 5-story *insula*.

"In there," pointed Stena. "He lives on the 3rd floor."

Vulso and Crantor went to the front door, while Stena stayed back with Severus. Vulso opened the front door and saw the *ianitor* seated just inside.

The doorman looked up at the two large men, one in the military uniform of the Urban Cohort and the other with muscles bulging his tunic. He jumped to his feet.

"Is Furius here?" asked Vulso.

"Maybe. I don't know. I just came on duty within the last hour."

"Take us to his apartment."

The *ianitor* led them up to the third floor and pointed out a door.

Vulso knocked. There was no answer. He knocked again. Again, no answer. He turned to the *ianitor*. "Open the door."

The *ianitor* selected a key from the keyring hanging from his belt and opened the door.

Vulso went in first and was the first to see the chaos. On a table was a cup of red wine and an over-turned wine bottle. On the floor behind the table there was a dead body. Next to the body, there was a cup on its side with wine partly drained from it and a scroll. The face of the body on the floor was contorted, in both surprise and distress. His eyes bulged, his tongue hung out.

"I don't see any wounds on him," said Crantor, kneeling down to inspect the body.

"Look at his eyes," commented Vulso. "He looks like he was poisoned," He sniffed the wine cup on the table and the overturned bottle of wine. Then he picked up the wine cup lying next to the dead man. "No smell. And I'm sure if he drank it, no strange taste. So probably arsenic. The cup left on the table is filled with wine. Someone else must have been here, someone who didn't drink the wine."

He turned to the *ianitor*. "Get the *ianitor* who was on duty before you."

Crantor went downstairs to tell Severus, who immediately came upstairs and looked over the scene. The other *ianitor* was already there. He was a scraggly old man who gave his name as Lollius. When he saw the scene he looked shocked, his palm to his mouth, his eyes wide open.

"Is that Furius?" asked Severus, pointing to the body.

The *ianitor* nodded yes.

"When did he come in today? Was anyone with him, or if not, did anyone come to see him?"

"He came in alone about the time of the afternoon siesta. I didn't see anyone come in asking for him. Only other residents of the *insula* came in and out." He thought for a moment. "But I wasn't at the door all the time. About an hour after Furius came in, a woman came to the front door and said she was lost, asking me for directions. She was a handsome woman with red hair and she got me to leave my post and go outside with her. She walked me down the street, asking where to go. It's possible someone came to see Furius while I was helping the woman. But I can't say for sure."

"Possibly, Lollius, you were deliberately distracted," replied the judge. "Did you see anyone leave, other than a resident?"

"I didn't really notice. I was seated reading a scroll. Generally, I notice if people come in or out, but only if they say something to me. This is terrible. Terrible. I should notify the owner."

"Who is the owner?"

"It's called the *Insula Papirius*. It was once owned by a member of the Senatorial Order, Titus Papirius Paculus. But I heard he lost the whole building in a dice game. I don't know who won it. All I know is that someone who says he is an agent of the new owner appears the first of every month to collect rents and pay me and the other slaves our slave salaries, our *peculium*."

Severus made a note to have Alexander go to the City Aedile's office first thing next morning and find out who is the registered owner of this *insula*. Then he picked up the scroll on the floor next to the body of Furius and unfurled it. He started reading, a look of surprise and glee on his face the further he read. When he finished, he let it unfurl and looked at Vulso and Crantor.

"Interesting. This scroll seems to be a chronological record of Furius' crimes, what they were, how much he was paid, and who hired him. The one at the top refers to the attempt to kill me. The one just before that notes the killing of the Whale."

"What does it say about who hired him?"

"It says 'Zeno' for both those crimes and for a few others as well."

"Zeno?" asked Vulso. "Isn't he the freedman of Senator Paculus? The one who is a business and personal rival of Antipater, the charterer of *Andromeda*? Isn't he the one Antipater, and Paculus too, accused of being involved in the *Andromeda* robbery?"

"Yes. It must be him. We never investigated him because, except for the accusations of Antipater and

Paculus, there wasn't a shred of evidence against him. No one we've questioned so far has even mentioned his name, except for Antipater and Paculus. But now, it seems, we have some evidence pointing to him as perhaps being *Ipse*.

"Obviously, I must question Zeno as soon as possible. Tomorrow morning. Vulso, find out where we can find him, take a few soldiers with you and bring him to my chambers under guard."

"I'll have him there at the 3rd hour."

"Good. The Tribunal will be set up. I'll question him from there."

XXX

ZENO IS QUESTIONED BEFORE THE TRIBUNAL

As promised, Vulso had Zeno before the Tribunal at the 3rd hour. The Tribunal, however, was not set up outdoors in public, but indoors in a courtroom inside the colonnade in the Forum of Augustus. This was only an inquiry, not a trial, so there was no requirement for a public session.

Zeno was placed in front of the Tribunal, with the judge looking down from his seat on the 4-foot-high platform. Zeno was a thin, short man perhaps 50 years old, with most of his hair gone, a barely discernable beard, and a scared and confused look on his face. Clearly, he did not know what had happened to him that morning from the time Vulso and three soldiers had arrived at his place of business and taken him into custody. He had asked a few times what was going on, why he had been taken, where he was going? Vulso told him to shut up. He was being taken before a special judge and would learn from him what it was about. Zeno shut up, but his face was at times not just worried, but terrified. Now Severus addressed him.

"State your name and status in society?"

"My name is Titus Paculanus Zeno. I am a Roman citizen, a freedman of Titus Papirius Paculus, a member of the Senatorial Order."

Severus decided to get straight to the point. He nodded to Vulso, who showed Zeno the painting of Furius. "How long have you known this man?"

Zeno looked at it and shook his head. "I don't know him at all. I've never seen him."

"You've never seen him? His name is Furius. And he works for you."

"He works for me? Not that I know of. There must be some mistake. Ask anyone in my home, in my business. I've never seen him before. If that's why I'm here, it's all a mistake. I'm being mistaken for someone else."

"This scroll names you as Furius' employer in crime. Did Furius make a mistake?"

Severus nodded to a lictor who handed the scroll to Zeno. Zeno unfurled it and read it. Then he let it furl up, handed it back to the lictor and addressed the Judge.

"I can't explain it, *eminentissime*. All I know is that I never employed this Furius for anything. I never met him and don't know him. That scroll must be a forgery. That's what it is. A forgery."

Severus turned to one of the lictors. "Take him out."

The lictor escorted Zeno out of the courtroom.

"He's lying," said Vulso. "He poisoned Furius and is covering up the fact that Furius was one of his thugs. He's *Ipse.*"

"Maybe he's not lying," replied Severus. "How do we know one way or the other."

"That scroll that we found next to the body of Furius says it all," answered Vulso. "It names Zeno as his employer for various crimes, including the attack on you, Judge."

"But suppose it is a forgery. I've been uncomfortable with the idea that a *grassator* like Furius would keep a record of his crimes and who hired him to do them. There's something fishy about that."

"Maybe it is fishy. But he could have recorded and kept a list of his crimes, just the same."

"I suppose so. But we have to find out one way or another." He turned to the lictor. "Bring back Zeno. As long as I have him here, there are a few other questions I have for him."

Zeno was brought back and placed in front of the Tribunal.

"We will find out whether you are telling the truth about knowing Furius. But I have a few other questions for you. First, tell me about your rivalry with Antipater."

"Antipater? Him I know, unfortunately. He stole my woman, for one thing. He tried to ruin my business, for another."

"How did he do that?"

"I'm also in the merchant shipping business, though he has a lot more businesses than I do, and not just in shipping. Still, he tries to undercut my prices, whenever he can. He also tried to prevent me from chartering ships by chartering them for himself whenever he found out I needed a ship."

"Did you try to charter the *Andromeda*?"

"No. I don't charter ships any more because of Antipater's interferences. I own my own merchant ship instead. As for the *Andromeda,* I will tell you forthrightly that I'm glad Antipater lost the ship and his cargo. I'm glad he lost so much money. I hate him, as he hates me."

"But you were once friends, weren't you?"

"Antipater is no one's friend, though he may pretend to be. He is only interested in himself."

"But you also invested a million sesterces in the shipment of silk on the *Andromeda*, didn't you? If you hated Antipater so much, why did you invest in his enterprise?"

Zeno looked sheepish. "I did invest my money with him. But it was a business decision, not a personal one. And while Antipater and I may hate each other, the silk cargo might have brought me a fortune. Now I will be hard put to regain what I have lost."

"Tell me about Senator Paculus. You are his freedman, aren't you?"

"Yes. I am. But he is a compulsive gambler, as everyone knows. That's all that interests him. Every time I go to his house to pay respects, all he wants to do is roll dice with me. I have to do it, naturally, because of his status. But he is not only a compulsive gambler, he is a lousy gambler. Somehow, he always loses. When he wins at dice, for instance, he always wants to continue until he loses. He doesn't know when to stop."

"Did he compel you and Antipater to roll dice for the woman you were both interested in?"

Zeno's face hardened. "Yes. That viper. I know he's of the Senatorial Order, but he's a viper. He made us roll dice for Cassandra because he wanted to see us suffer. Not only me and Antipater, but Cassandra too. She was a slave, it's true, and had been his concubine, but rolling dice for her was a deliberate humiliation. And we had no choice. Even though we were free, we were his clients, he our patron."

"Do you know Octavia, his cousin?"

"Of course. She and he are lovers. They were once quite close. They did everything together. But his gambling has now taken over and I don't know how she can reach him anymore. I don't know for sure, of course. You'll have to ask them."

"You'll be put in a cell until your story of a forgery is either confirmed or disproven. If the first, you will be released. If the second, I need not elucidate the harsh consequences now."

XXXI

THE INVESTIGATION CONTINUES

The next morning Severus sent out his entourage to investigate specific issues.

Vulso was sent to the *Insula Paculus*, where Furius lived and was murdered, to talk to its residents about Furius. In particular, they were to try to find a sample of Furius' handwriting. Either by searching his room or by talking to residents, they might find something Furius wrote. Perhaps letters, messages, even notes. If they could obtain a copy of Furius' handwriting, then a comparison with the scroll that named Zeno as his employer in crime could be made.

By the same token, Straton was to go to Zeno's place of business and obtain a copy of his handwriting, so that a comparison could be made.

Alexander was sent to the office of the City Aedile to find out who now owned the *Insula Paculus*. Did Paculus actually lose it in a dice game to someone who now owned it? If so, who to?

As for Octavia and Paculus, handwriting samples from them could wait until they were garnered from Furius and Zeno.

They all left to carry out their missions. Severus stayed in his chambers to await results. He picked up a book he was reading. Actually re-reading. It was the book of Lucian called *A True History* about a war between the inhabitants of the Sun and the inhabitants of the Moon over colonizing Venus. The Sun-ites rode giant winged ants; the moon-ites giant vultures. Both sides had allies coming from the stars. This book always stimulated Severus' imagination and took his mind off earthly things, like who *Ipse* was.

Alexander was the first to return and report.

"The *Insula Pacula* was no longer registered to Titus Paculus as the owner, but was now owned by someone named Publius Manilius Balbus. Balbus lives at an address on the Esquiline Hill. Should we interview him?

"Let's wait and see what Vulso and Straton find out."

Straton was the next to return. He had succeeded in obtaining what purported to be a few samples of Zeno's handwriting from business correspondence, both on scrolls and in waxed tablets. He also had shown the painting of Furius around to workers in Zeno's office, but no one admitted to knowing him. They all wanted to know what was happening to Zeno.

"I put them off, of course. I told them that we were making routine inquiries and copies of his handwriting would be valuable. I told them Zeno wanted us to have them."

Vulso returned an hour later.

"Did you get any handwriting sample of Furius?" asked the judge straight off.

"No."

"No? Why not?"

"Because I found out from a neighbor, who is a scribe, that Furius was illiterate. He could neither read nor write. There are therefore no handwriting samples. I showed him the scroll supposedly written by Furius. He said he didn't recognize the handwriting. But of course, it couldn't have been written by Furius because he didn't know how to write."

"So obviously this scroll is a forgery," concluded Severus.

"Not necessarily," continued Vulso, hesitantly, making it up as he went along. "Furius could have… No. That doesn't make much sense."

"What were you about to say?"

"I was thinking that Furius could have dictated it to someone who wrote it down for him. The scribe I talked to said Furius used him whenever he wanted something written, but he didn't write this scroll." Vulso sounded more unconvinced as he expounded the theory. "No. You're right, Judge. Why would a *grassator* dictate his crimes and name his criminal boss to someone else. Usually *grassatores* conceal their crimes, not make them public."

Severus had a broad smile on his face. "Gather everyone at the Praefectura tomorrow morning at the 3rd hour. I now know who *Ipse* is. And I will reveal who it is then."

"When you say everyone," asked Vulso. "Who do you mean?"

"All of us, naturally. Vulso, Straton, Crantor, Alexander, Proculus, Artemisia and Flaccus. I also want the Urban Prefect to be present. Also, I want judge Sulpicius to be there. Then I want Titus Paculus, Octavia, Zeno, Antipater, the charterer of *Andromeda* and Opimius, the owner of *Andromeda*. In the wings in case I need them, I want Felix, the henchman of the Whale and the recruiter of robbers, Atrox, the robber chief, Scylax and Baaldo, the officers of the *Andromeda*, and Demetrios, the Captain of the *Andromeda*. Oh, and I want the *ianitor* of the *Insula Paculus* where Furius was murdered. Lollius, I think his name is. I think that should do it."

"I'll send out the appropriate messages and messengers," said Proculus.

"I'll send out some soldiers with the messengers, to see that no one holds back," said Vulso.

"And Vulso," said Severus almost as an afterthought, "there is one other person I want to be here. But I'll tell you about that tomorrow morning."

Severus then picked up his *A True History* and headed for the door. "I'm going to have dinner, read more of my book tonight and get a good night's sleep. Tomorrow will be a fateful day."

XXXII

IPSE REVEALED

The courtroom at the Praefectura was set up for the session the next morning. Judge Severus was on the center of the Tribunal, seated on the magistrate's camp chair. On his right was the Urban Prefect himself, Lucius Sergius Paullus, and to his right Quintus Proculus, taking down the proceedings in shorthand. To Severus' left was Judge Sulpicius, and to his left Gaius Flaccus, Severus' assessor.

In the semi-circle of seats in front of the Tribunal were, on the Tribunal's left, Vulso, Straton, Crantor, Alexander and Artemisia. On the Tribunal's right were Senator Titus Paculus and Octavia Prisca, then a space and then Antipater, Zeno and Opimius. These five faced the Tribunal with varying feelings of confidence and trepidation, though their expressions generally did not reflect whatever feelings they had. Each projected, to one degree or another, an almost child-like expression of innocence.

Lictors stood against the wall behind the Tribunal, with their bundle of rods. The bust of Jupiter Fidius stood solidly in the front of the courtroom.

Severus began.

"We are here to expose *Ipse*, the criminal behind the wrecking of the merchant ship *Andromeda*, the theft of its cargo of silk from *Seres* and the murder of various passengers and crew who got in the way.

"What happened is now clear. The ship *Andromeda*, on its way from Alexandria to Rome, was owned by Opimius and chartered for this voyage by Antipater, who owned its extremely valuable cargo of *serica* silk.

"The expenses of the purchase of the silk in Alexandria and the voyage to bring it to Rome were in part met by investors who hoped to reap huge profits with a successful conclusion to the voyage. These investors, besides the normal *argentarii* bankers, and *negotiatores* professional investors, included some private investors. Among these were Titus Paculus, for a million sesterces, Octavia for half a million, Opimius for a million, Zeno for a million sesterces and Judge Sulpicius for half a million."

Judge Sulpicius sat up in surprise at the mention of his name. As did the Urban Prefect, who turned to his left and looked at Judge Sulpicius in astonishment.

"Is this true?" asked the Urban Prefect, addressing Judge Sulpicius. Before he could answer, Judge Severus motioned to his court clerk who pulled a document out of a *capsa* at his feet and handed it to the Urban Prefect.

"That," explained Severus, "is the list of investors in the *Andromeda* enterprise from the files of

Antipater. You will see Septimus Sosius Sulpicius, Judge Sulpicius, listed among them for half a million sesterces."

"But you," said the Prefect looking at Judge Sulpicius, "you presided at the trial of Demetrios, the Captain of the *Andromeda*. To my mind that is a clear conflict of interest. You should have recused yourself under these circumstances."

Judge Sulpicius started to say something. "But, I...."

The Prefect held up his hand to curtail whatever Sulpicius was about to say and made a statement instead. "Judge Sulpicius, you are hereby removed from the panel of judges in the Court of the Urban Prefect and consequently I order you to get off this Tribunal. Now."

Sulpicius got up hesitantly, and with everyone staring at him, left the courtroom.

"There's no room in my court for judges like that," commented the Prefect.

"Exactly my sentiments," agreed Severus, with a smile.

Then he continued. "I was talking about the investors in the *Andromeda* voyage and mentioned, besides Sulpicius, all five of you seated in front to my right. Of you five, the greatest investor who had the most to gain or lose was, of course, Antipater, the charterer of the ship, who owned the silk from *Seres*. But all you others, Paculus, Octavia, Opimius and Zeno also lost substantial amounts of money. So if you all lost money, how could any of you profit, how could any of you be *Ipse*? The answer in short is that the robbery of the *Andromeda* was committed not to gain money, but to cause others to lose it. Money was not the motive, personal hatred was."

"To prove this, I will reconstruct what happened. First, the *Andromeda* sailed from Rome to Alexandria with a cargo of wine, *terra sigilata* pottery, glassware and other trade goods. Its Captain was Demetrios, an employee of the owner Opimius. He commanded the ship at sea. There were two other officers aboard, both of whom were employees of Antipater. These were the Shipmaster Scylax and the First Mate, Baaldo. These officers, by the way, had previously worked not only for Antipater, but also for Opimius and for Zeno.

There was in addition a crew of 200 hundred and about 200 passengers. On the return voyage from Alexandria to Rome, there was the same number of crew and passengers and a cargo of oil, lentils, wine, wheat and Alexandrian glass. But above all was the most valuable cargo, silk from *Seres*, worth many, many millions.

'The weather was good, as it was in the middle of the sailing season. But one night, as the ship came up the coast of Italy nearing Ostia, the port of Rome, a short distance past Laurentum it suddenly veered toward the shore and ran aground. The place where this happened had been lighted up by torches already there, showing the way. The torches were displayed by the band of robbers headed by Atrox. He knew where to be when the ship was off shore because accomplices on the ship had regularly signaled by semaphore to other accomplices on land about the ship's progress toward Ostia. So that night the robbers on shore signaled to their accomplices on the ship with torches just where the ship should be beached.

"Once the signal torches were seen on the ship, the conspirators on board, Scylax and Baaldo, killed the man at the tiller and themselves turned the rudder oars to direct the ship onto land. While one of them, probably Scylax, manned the rudders, the other, Baaldo, slugged Captain Demetrios as he came out of his cabin to investigate what was happening.

"Once *Andromeda* was on shore, the robbers cut down anyone who got in the way and took off the cargo of silk, put it aboard coaches they had with them and drove away to Rome, taking their accomplices from the ship, Scylax and Baaldo, with them.

"When reports reached Rome the next morning, troops of the Urban Cohort were sent to investigate. They rounded up a number of the robbers, particularly those who had been recruited as stevedores and left to their own devices to reach Rome on foot. A payoff, they had been told, would be given them two months after the robbery, after the loot was sold. The payoff would take place in Taurus' *taberna* in the Subura and would be made to those who gave the password 'Ajax'.

"From information gleaned from robbers who were captured, among others, it soon became clear that the plot for this robbery was hatched in an *insula* in the Subura, the *Insula Octavia*. At the center of the criminal enterprise was a fulltime resident of this *insula* named Balaena, the Whale, an immensely obese person. He had met with Atrox, the robber chief, he directed Felix, another resident of the *insula*, to recruit stevedores, and he organized the plan along with

Scylax and Baaldo, the two ship's officers who also resided in the *Insula Octavia.*

"But while all these conspirators took their directions from the Whale, the Whale purportedly took his orders from the real mastermind, who was called *Ipse,* 'Himself', just like the Emperor is called *Ipse* by his court, or the head of an academy by his underlings. *Ipse* carefully concealed his identity. No one but the Whale knew it.

"How do we know that the story about *Ipse* is not a fictional one. That the Whale was not taking orders from *Ipse*, but was *Ipse* himself.

"The answer is provided by the fact that the Whale was murdered. When he was facing imminent capture by me and my assistants, he was eliminated. Clearly, he was killed by someone who feared being exposed by the Whale. And who could that be but *Ipse*. *Ipse* sent Furius to murder me, then to murder the Whale and then he murdered Furius,shortly thereafter. So there was in fact a real person, *Ipse,* who gave orders to the Whale.

"But who is *Ipse*?" Severus asked rhetorically and looked at the five people seated in front and to the right of the Tribunal.

"It is one of you five," he said. "Why one of you? Because each of you had a connection with Scylax and Baaldo and the Whale, who we know were participants and developers of the crime. Both Scylax and Baaldo worked at various times for Antipater, Opimius and Zeno. Octavia, of course, was directly connected to the Whale because he ran things for her at the *Insula Octavia.* And Paculus was intimately connected to Octavia.

"But while all of you had connections that can be traced to the Whale, which one is *Ipse*? A Roman judge in a court case is trained to ask the question, *cui bono*? To who's good? Who profits? Who has a motive?

"Here, however, it seems that everyone loses money. Antipater lost his extremely valuable cargo. Opimius lost his ship and his investment. Zeno lost his investment. Titus Paculus and Octavia also lost substantial investments. *Cui bono*?"

Severus paused to take a drink. Then he continued. "The idea that whoever lost financially could not be behind the crime is a logical one. But it occurred to me that in this case, it is wrong. The motive of *Ipse* here was not to gain riches for himself, but to ruin his enemies. It was not to make himself richer, but to make others poorer. And at one stroke he accomplished that by turning the voyage of the *Andromeda* from a huge success into a dismal failure where all his enemies were ruined.

Severus looked at Antipater with probing eyes and addressed him directly. "Antipater, you are Zeno's rival. You and he hate each other. Is that not true?"

"Rather say, *eminentissime*," replied Antipater, "that he is my rival than the other way around. I married Cassandra, the woman who Zeno wanted. Zeno hates me for that. I do not hate him. So, yes, there is a rivalry, but I am not the instigator, he is."

"Antipater, besides Zeno, there are others here who you have personal animus against. Paculus, for one. Don't you try to lord it over him? Don't you try to show him that you are better than him, despite the disparate status in society between him and you? Aren't you motivated to in effect change places with him as master and slave? Don't you want to ruin him?"

"You are talking nonsense, *eminentissime.* I pay off his gambling debts. If I wanted to ruin him, why would I do that?"

"What about Octavia? Don't you have personal animus against her for denying you the beautiful girl Persephone? Didn't you want to buy her and weren't you angry and stymied when Octavia forestalled you by freeing her?"

"This is again nonsense. Persephone is a beautiful girl, yes. But I can have as many beautiful girls as I want. I can buy them by the dozens."

"And what about Opimius? Don't you want to ruin him out of personal animus? Don't you two hate each other, not only as business rivals, but personally?

"What I am saying Antipater, is that while you may have lost financially by the wreckage of the *Andromeda*, you gained personally by ruining your enemies, Paculus, Octavia, Zeno and Opimius. Wasn't revenge against your enemies your real motive for committing this crime? Didn't you see this crime as a way to ruin all your enemies at one stroke. It wasn't money that moved you, Antipater. You are wealthy enough to absorb or recoup any financial loss from the wreck and robbery of the *Andromeda.* It was personal hatred and revenge that motivated you. You are *Ipse.*"

"*Nugax.* Nonsense," objected Antipater forcefully. "I deny your accusation. Your fanciful theories are not evidence."

"So you say. But I have one piece of evidence that you can't deny and that is conclusive that you poisoned Furius and that you are *Ipse*."

Antipater almost laughed and sarcastically challenged the Judge. "Oh, and what is that, *eminentissime*?"

Severus turned to one of the lictors. "Bring in that old man, Lollius."

The lictor went out and came back with the scraggly old doorkeeper of the *insula* where Furius was murdered and placed him before the Tribunal.

"What is your name and occupation?"

"My name is Lollius and I am the *ianitor* of the *Insula Paculus*."

"Is that the *insula* where Furius lived?"

"It is."

"Were you on duty on the day Furius was murdered?"

"I was."

"Did you see Furius come back home that afternoon?"

"I did."

"Did you see whether anyone visited him?"

"I saw no one who came in asking for him."

"Were you on duty all the time that afternoon?"

"Yes, except for one incident when a young woman came by saying she was lost and got me to go with her down the street to help her find her way."

"Did you get a good look at that woman?"

"Yes."

"How would you describe her?"

"She was very good looking and had red hair."

"Do you think you could identify her if you saw her again?"

"Yes. No question."

"Thank you, Lollius. You may go to the holding room."

When he left, Severus turned to Zeno.

"Zeno, the woman Cassandra who you wanted to marry, but who married Antipater. How would you describe her?"

Zeno looked at Antipater with a hostile glare. "Cassandra is notable for her beautiful long red hair."

"Antipater," said Severus. "Stand up."

He stood.

"Do you want me to bring Cassandra here to be identified by the doorkeeper?"

Antipater stayed silent, glaring at the judge.

"While you had Cassandra distract the doorman at the *Insula Paculus*, you snuck in and went to Furius' room with a bottle of poisoned wine. You gave him a glassful which he drank and died. Then you put that scroll which you had forged into his hand as he lay on the floor dying. In it you named Zeno in an attempt to frame him. You are *Ipse*. You committed this crime to ruin all your enemies. To break Paculus for good, to get back at Octavia for thwarting your attempt to buy Persephone, to get back at Zeno on account of your rivalry with him, to ruin Opimius as well. That's the truth, isn't it, *Ipse*?"

Antipater remained mute. Then he replied.

"I want my lawyer. Get me Septimus Eggius. He'll make mincemeat out of your so-called theory. I want my lawyer and I want a trial."

"You'll get both Antipater. But first, I want your wife Cassandra to come here now and be identified. I'm sure you won't want to miss that, Antipater. We'll all wait together."

They didn't have long to wait. She had been brought to the Forum of Augustus by Vulso that morning after Antipater had left for court. A lictor brought her into the courtroom. She looked around with wonder and confusion, seeing her husband and then Zeno, and then Paculus. She was turned and placed in front of the Tribunal.

She had long red hair. It drew stares from everyone.

Lollius, the doorman at the *Insula Paculus* was then brought in. He took one look at Cassandra and spoke to the Judge on the Tribunal.

"That's her. No doubt about it. That's the woman who came to the *insula* and told me she was lost. She got me to walk down the street away from my post. That's her, all right. No doubt about it."

"Thank you, Lollius." Severus turned to Cassandra. "It was you, wasn't it, who was at the *Insula Paculus* that day, who distracted the doorman so that your husband Antipater could sneak inside without being seen?"

Cassandra looked at Antipater and then back at the Judge and then at Antipater again. She saw Paculus and Zeno as well, and her look of confusion turned into a look of understanding, lighting up her face and eyes. She understood what was going on. A scowl then was on her face as she turned toward her husband. A smile displaced it when she looked at the Judge.

"Yes, it was me, Judge. That monster who calls himself my husband," here she turned at glared at Antipater and spoke directly to him, "you viper. I hate you. I hate you more than I've ever hated anyone." Then she turned toward Titus Paculus, her former master, and pointed a finger at him. "And I hate you too. You abused me as your slave. You took advantage of me as a young girl. You gave me away on a throw of dice. I would hate you the most of everyone, if I didn't hate that monster Antipater more." She turned back to the Judge.

"Yes, Antipater got me to distract the doorman. He snuck into that building. He never told me why. I still don't know why. I only see that he must have done something wrong or he wouldn't be here and Paculus wouldn't be here and I wouldn't be here. I hope you get him, Judge. I hope you sentence him to death in the arena, to be torn apart by monsters like himself." Her whole being emanated hatred and satisfaction.

"Your hope may be fulfilled," replied Severus, and concluded the court session.

EPILOGUE

MARCUS FLAVIUS
SEVERUS: TO HIMSELF

Antipater got his lawyer and his trial. Neither did him much good. He was tried along with Scylax, the Shipmaster, and Baaldo, the First Mate. Felix, the confederate of the Whale, who did recruiting for him and proffered the stolen silks for sale was also a co-defendant at their trial.

The robbers, Atrox the chief of the gang, and those who were arrested after receiving their pay at Taurus' *taberna*, including Aures, 'Ears', who cooperated, were defendants at a separate trial, along the two assassins, Kastor and Borvo, who tried to kill me in the park.

Others, like Hector, who had been recruited as a 'stevedore' off the streets of Rome without knowing what he was getting into, and who cooperated with my investigation, were not put on trial at all.

I presided over the trial of Antipater, Scylax, Baaldo and Felix. Another judge, Judge Memmius, presided over the trial of everyone else. I thought there would be a conflict of interest if I were to preside over the criminals who tried to kill me.

In truth, it hardly mattered. Everyone was convicted at both trials of crimes ranging from stealing a ship, to murder, to robbery, to selling stolen goods.

As for sentencing, I sentenced Antipater, Scylax, Baaldo and Felix all to death. Antipater was the mastermind, the others deeply implicated accomplices in the crimes. My only hesitation was over the manner of their deaths. I could order death by being thrown to wild beasts in the arena or by crucifixion, by strangling, or being thrown from a height, by drowning or being whipped to death. The most honorable and quickest death was beheading.

I didn't think these were honorable criminals. But Scylax, Baaldo and Felix were not Roman citizens and therefore were not entitled to be beheaded. Rather, they were subject to be killed by any of these cruel punishments. On the other hand, Antipater was a Roman citizen by virtue of his having been freed from slavery to a Roman citizen. He was therefore entitled to be beheaded. But the question I asked myself was how could I justify sentencing these others to a more horrible death than the arch-criminal himself? I didn't see how I could. I discussed it with Artemisia, with Vulso, Straton, Crantor, Alexander and Proculus. We all agreed that it would be unjust to sentence the most guilty to the least onerous death, while sentencing the others to the most horrible deaths. Accordingly, I sentenced them all to be beheaded.

As for Atrox, the robber chief, he was sentenced by Judge Memmius *ad bestias*, to death by wild beasts in the arena, as were most of his robber band. The ones who cooperated, like Ears, and the assassins who tried to kill me, Kastor and Borvo, they were sentenced *ad metallum*, to the mines, where they would probably die anyway.

Demetrios, the Captain of the *Andromeda*, who was tortured into confessing, and wrongfully convicted by Judge Sulpicius, won his appeal to the Urban Prefect and was set free, though still a mental and physical wreck

Judge Sulpicius, who convicted Demetrios and turned the other way when he was tortured into confessing, was prosecuted under the Cornelian Law as a magistrate in a criminal case who convicted an innocent person using false testimony. Disgraced, and facing the Cornelian Law penalty for upper class *honestiores* of exile to an island and confiscation of all his property, Sulpicius opened his veins and killed himself.

So at the conclusion of the trials, I was at last free to return to my retirement home in the Alban hills. And that's exactly where I went, along with Artemisia, Flavia, Quintus and Argos. Alexander, however, decided to stay in Rome, still smitten by Persephone.

Back in the countryside, I resumed studying the stars and planets, along with Quintus, who also delved further into geometry and mathematics, while Artemisia continued writing her biography of Aspasia. Flavia recovered slowly from her depression, helped along by writing poems and playing music on her cithara.

Was there a better life than that? For the children, yes, because they still had to grow and mature, marry and raise a family. But for Artemisia and myself, we were content, still together and in love, and were each doing creative and interesting work. What more could we ask?

HISTORICAL NOTE

The silk trade between Rome and China and Roman commerce with the East is the subject of a number of excellent studies. I found most interesting Raoul McLaughlin, *The Roman Empire and the Silk Routes* (Pen and Sword, 2016); Berit Hildebrandt ed., *Silk: Trade and Exchange along the Silk Roads between Rome and China in Antiquity* (Oxbow books, 2017); G.F. Hudson, *Europe and China*, (Beacon Press, 1931); Raoul McLaughlin, *The Roman Empire and the Indian Ocean,* (Pen and Sword, 2014).

Also, there is still extent the anonymous *Periplus Maris Erythraei*, (Sailing around the Red Sea). This is a work of the 2nd century CE that describes trade from ports in Roman Egypt, India, the Persian Gulf and surrounding areas.

Roman merchant ships, their construction, their crews, and everything else about them, are thoroughly treated in Lionel Casson, *Ships and Seamanship in the Ancient World* (Princeton Univ. Press 1971); also see, Cecil Torr, *Ancient Ships* (Chicago 1964), among other works and web sites.

The picture of the Roman merchant ship on the cover is from a carving on a sarcophagus in the Mariner's Museum, Newport News, Virginia. Another similar one is in the National Museum in Beirut. On the web, the ship is confusingly called a Phoenician ship. But it is clearly a Roman cargo ship of the 2nd century CE, as it is properly identified in Casson, *supra*, illustration 156; Cecil Torr, *supra,* plate DD.

The description of the shipwreck of the *Andromeda* is based primarily on Paul's New Testament report of his own shipwreck in Acts: 27.

Information about ancient Roman paleontology and Roman museum exhibits of giant bones comes primarily from Adrienne Mayor, *"The First Fossil Hunters"* (Princeton Univ. Press 2000).

Roman law schools are discussed in *"The Study of Roman Law – Roman Law Schools,"* by Charles P. White, 17 Yale Law Journal 499-512 (May 1908).

Interestingly, the split in outlook between the law school of Proculus and the law school of Sabinus is between conservatives and liberals. The conservative Proculeans advocated keeping to original legal formulas, while the liberal Sabinians advocated modifying outdated legalisms to keep up with changing times. Sound familiar?

For Plato on the equal education and equality of women, see Rep. V .451c – 452; 454d – e. On the philosophic nature of dogs, Rep. II. 376

For more details on the Antonine plague, see the Judge Severus mystery, *Mission to Athens* and its historical note at the end. The 'miasma theory' that disease is caused by pollution in the air persisted from ancient times until it was replaced by the germ theory of disease in the 19th century. The disease 'malaria', which at one time was prevalent in ancient Rome, literally means 'bad air.'

Once again, I would like to thank Ruth Chevion for her careful and insightful editing, her excellent suggestions and useful discussions about the book. I continue to thank her especially for her loving care, support and encouragement over many years.

Printed in Great Britain
by Amazon

27868614R00157